About the Author

Lawrence Stellato Sr. was born, raised, and educated in New York. After three careers as an executive in publishing, a business owner, and a property owner and manager, he decided to devote his remaining time to a long-held desire to put into print a lifetime of ideas. His first book, *Past, Present, and Future of Planet Earth,* is an insightful speculation on the growth of intelligent life on Earth. *Love Letters to America* is intended to illustrate his great admiration and respect for our democracy and capitalist society.

Love Letters to America

Lawrence Stellato Sr.

Love Letters to America

Olympia Publishers
London

www.olympiapublishers.com
OLYMPIA PAPERBACK EDITION

Copyright © Lawrence Stellato Sr. 2024

The right of Lawrence Stellato Sr. to be identified as author of
this work has been asserted in accordance with sections 77 and 78 of
the Copyright, Designs and Patents Act 1988.

All Rights Reserved

No reproduction, copy or transmission of this publication
may be made without written permission.
No paragraph of this publication may be reproduced,
copied or transmitted save with the written permission of the publisher,
or in accordance with the provisions
of the Copyright Act 1956 (as amended).

Any person who commits any unauthorized act in relation to
this publication may be liable to criminal
prosecution and civil claims for damage.

A CIP catalogue record for this title is
available from the British Library.

ISBN: 978-1-80439-798-5

The opinions expressed in this book are the author's own and do not
reflect the views of the publisher, author's employer, organization,
committee or other group or individual.

First Published in 2024

Olympia Publishers
Tallis House
2 Tallis Street
London
EC4Y 0AB

Printed in Great Britain

Dedication

To Barbara... the inspiration for the title and cover.

Introduction

Let it never be said that I have lost my love for everything that the United States of America stands for. Never let it be said that I could ever be convinced that the original constitution and country created by our original founding fathers were ever intended by them to be changed into what exists today. Before my earliest education, I was taught that we lived in the greatest society ever created by mankind, and everything I have learned since about American and world history has only confirmed that belief in my mind.

Great efforts are being made today by many wealthy and powerful people to convince all people worldwide that the United States of America has been, since its inception, evil and dedicated to taking advantage of all of mankind. They would convince us that American capitalism creates wealth for the few who enslave the masses, but neglect to mention that their wealth, which they have no intention of giving up, came from American capitalism. It was never the intention of capitalism to create the greed that exists among billionaires and in corporations today. The capitalist system is not the reason people are as greedy as they are or the reason that governments interfere with the system and stunt economic growth. They would have us believe that the Western European nations and America, which embraced democracy and capitalism, had economies that flourished by stealing natural resources from poorer nations and failing to share the wealth. They fail to mention that it was America and Western Europe that invented all energy creation and the industrial revolution, which showered all the nations of the world that accepted it with a substantially improved way of life. They fail to mention that the purchase of oil for energy needs in the United States and Western Europe has enriched many countries around the world. They fail to mention the middle-class wealth that has been accumulated by so many of America's trading partners and those of Western Europe. Would a nation dedicated to taking advantage of the world have sacrificed so much to help the world defeat Germany in its effort for European domination in World War I? Would a nation dedicated to taking advantage of the world have sacrificed so much to help keep Germany and Japan from world domination in World War II?

There can be no question in my mind that the original intention of our founding fathers in the late 1700s when they created this country was to grant freedom and opportunity to the American people that had never existed anywhere on planet Earth previously throughout history. They fully understood what was happening in the world at the time and were dedicated to creating a life for the American people that contained freedoms no other people or nation had ever seen before. Who could argue that it was not democracy and capitalism that allowed the creation of every invention that improved the lives of everyone on the planet? And who could argue that it was the country created by our founding fathers that allowed democracy and capitalism to be born? An argument certainly can be made that these same opportunities and freedoms that were intended are not all still here today and that many of them are stifled by an overbearing government that was never intended by our founding fathers to have the power it has today.

It is my love for this great nation that was intended by

our forefathers that inspired me to write the love letters to America that I have included in this book. If you read them, I think you will understand my appreciation for being born in the nation that was created by these wonderful people who hoped that their ideas would benefit us all. I will love and cherish these ideals forever, and it is my hope that publishing these letters will reinject in our minds the desire to recreate America as it was intended to be and inspire many other nations on the planet to improve the lives of their own people.

Each of these letters is intended to address a particular issue that appears to be in contrast with a particular principle related to religion, economics, or social structure intended in the original creation of our government or society. Many of the letters relate to ways in which our government appears to be making policy that is not in the best interest of the American people. The dates of the letters often coincide with problems occurring at the time they were written. Many of them contain some sensible direction toward a reasonable solution or outcome.

Prologue

In my first book, titled *Past, Present, and Future of Planet Earth*, I speculate about the origin of intelligent life on our planet and attempt to trace the history of mankind on Earth. It contains a discussion of religions, which are our earliest history and the original source of all ethics and morality. It traces the growth of mankind into groups, societies, kingdoms, and then nations and alliances. The transition from kingdoms to societies where people have the right to elect their own rulers is discussed. We follow growth in types of government, economics, trade and the effects of these on the lives of nations, states, and people. The book is conservative in nature and critical of the tendency of government to be overbearing and to interfere in economies with negative consequences. I was born and raised in the United States and have always been a student of changes in society, government, economic and trade practices here more so than in other countries. As a result, a lot of the discussion in the book relates to U.S. policy and how it affects us and other countries. I have created a number of new economic principles that are conservative in nature and are covered in the book as well.

After writing this book, I realized that I have traced the course of intelligent life on planet Earth, but, although it is mentioned, I failed to articulate how strongly I feel that the planet is headed in the wrong direction in so many ways. It seems that so many of our leaders would like to eliminate religion from our lives. Perhaps they feel that the government should make the rules we live by instead of God. Governments seem to be encouraging the growth of technology that has the capability to enable our leaders to have more complete control over our lives. Do we want to live in a society where our government knows where each of us is at all times, knows every dollar we have, and knows where we are going every minute? That capability is practically already here. Do we want our government to have total ownership of all property and means of production? More than half of the population of the world is already living under that type of government control. Whether we are totally aware of it or not, in the entire history of the world, how much control our leaders have over us has always been what life and politics are all about. Even here in the United States, we have never been Democrats or Republicans. We have never been Liberals or Conservatives. It has always been about how much control we want the government to have over our lives. Democrats and Liberals have always voted for higher taxes, a larger government, and more control over our lives by our leaders. Conservatives and Republicans (for the most part) have always voted for less taxes, a smaller government, and more freedom from government control. During my lifetime at least, Democrats and Liberals have ruled our government for the most part, and we are losing the battle for control over our own lives that was intended by our forefathers. Wars always got in the way and tended to destroy economic progress for the people, but in the 1950s, I had the privilege to watch the unfolding of the greatest gift ever given to mankind. Inventions were being created everywhere because invention was rewarded, and all young people were achieving success and creating for themselves lives that were better than their parents. The entire world wanted to buy American products. We were witnessing the promise of our forefathers, who set the stage for the creation of the world's greatest society. Whether it was because of jealousy, greed, or whatever reason, in the 1960s, we began a great change in direction. We began to implement rules to stifle this great movement and try to return the nation and, as a result, the world to stagnation. Part of the problem was that we had to fight wars to attempt to stop the military spread of communism around the world. But we raised taxes to stifle economic progress based on the premise that the government had the right to redistribute wealth from the middle class to the poor. We created laws to eliminate the capability to hire the most competent people to create our products. Higher taxes, new laws on labor, and stronger unions inspired our corporations, which were the backbone of this great economy, to send manufacturing and later many headquarters overseas, eliminating so many opportunities for our young people. Increasing government control ever since has stunted economic growth until I do not believe we have any economic growth in the United States any more. Trade deals sent millions of jobs overseas. Most people believe that the Federal Reserve Bank actually controls the American economy today. The Federal Reserve does not control the economy, but it does take actions that appear to violate economic principles and stunt economic growth. Surely, we make fewer things in our country today than were made here many years ago. Surely, a much smaller percentage of our working-age population is employed today than a few years ago. If we truly eliminate inflation, surely our economy is smaller today. Surely, our government at all levels is way too large to be supported by our local economy. We have borrowed $30 trillion just on a national level alone. How long can we continue to live on borrowed money? The United States we live in today should be called by another name. It is not even close to what it was intended to be by our forefathers, which was actually coming to realization in the 1950s. In addition, today we have the New World Order, which is a global conspiracy to unite the world under the control of the United Nations. This globalization effort has no intention that the people of the world will have the freedoms and lifestyles intended by our forefathers in America. Not only is it intended that the governance of America would have to be subjugated to the United Nations, but the level of control that is intended over the people is more tyrannical than communism. We would only have to study the level of government control in China today to see what is intended. China has a central bank digital currency, which allows the government to know every dollar that you have and control your money and your life. The current administration in the United States is currently studying how to install a central bank digital currency here in the United States right now. It is worthy of note here that most of our recent presidents and heads of the departments of our government at the present time here in this country have been and are supporters of the New World Order. With the exception of Ronald Reagan and Donald Trump, this includes all recent presidents since Jimmy Carter. The Bush family, the Clintons, the Obamas, and the Bidens are certainly all supporters and would subjugate the United States to the United Nations.

After the completion of my book, I began to write articles, many of which covered topics that were in the book, and attempted to get them published in certain liberal and conservative publications. All of them were intended to respond to problems which were being discussed in the media at the time they were written and are therefore dated. I continue to believe that, if read by a large segment of our population, these articles could help to achieve a better understanding of the problems we face on planet Earth and give us some semblance of direction in arriving at some solutions. As suggested by the New World Order, the population of the planet is too large to achieve a dramatically improved life for everyone on the planet. In my opinion, this is the only thing the believers in the New World Order are correct about. They just do not have the correct solution. Governments everywhere are too large and too powerful. We have lost vision of true conservative economic principles which, if operated freely and without government interference, would improve our lives. We do need capitalism and the freedom provided by a democratic republic to provide for the continued improvement of life on Earth. Above all, we need to eliminate the thing that has always been the worst problem on planet Earth has always had... rich and powerful people who think they have the right to control all things and tell everyone else what to do and how to live. Instead, we must find a way to convince them to support ideas that will contribute to a truly better way of life for all on our planet. They are the ones that have the power to help make it happen.

These articles that I wrote have become my letters to the American people. They are intended to present to America the many ways that I believe the world is drifting so far in so many wrong directions and to show the ways in which America is also participating in this dangerous misdirection. It is intended to demonstrate how far we have drifted away from the freedoms and economic foundation that were created and intended for us by our founding fathers, and how much we have allowed our government to gain control over our daily lives, which was never intended. I hope that reading these letters will help many Americans become aware of the many mistakes we are making and develop some understanding of how we might begin to reestablish America in its original intended image.

Love Letter #1:
Supply Shortages and Rising Cost

October 20, 2021

Dear America,

It is my belief that the impact of trade policy on the lives of everyday working people is not well enough understood and more should be written about it. The content of this letter is mentioned in my first book, titled *Past, Present, and Future of Planet Earth*, which is available on Barnes and Noble and Amazon in paperback and e-book. I hope this will shed some light on a complicated subject for you.

There is a great deal of discussion today about shortages in the supply of goods and the increases in inflation that they are causing. Prices are rising for everything we need and buy every day, and more and more we are seeing empty shelves in supermarkets and department stores. Much of the blame is placed on the supply chain, the lack of capability to get product on shore from overseas manufacturers, and economic shutdowns due to the Covid 19 virus. We could argue all day about whether the virus necessitated a worldwide economic shutdown. It was and is not much worse than the flu, in my opinion, but the fact of the matter is that many countries did shut down their economies and are attempting to enforce other drastic measures. What I have not read a single article about is how we got to this point in the first place. How did we come to be so dependent on other countries for everything we eat, drink, wear, and use?

I was born in 1939. After World War II, as a young man, I remember that the United States had developed incredible manufacturing and agricultural capability and every country in the world wanted to buy American-made products. Our suppliers in America were capable of producing everything we needed here and what was sent overseas, but were stretched to do so. But supply and demand remained in balance, capital was available, and inflation remained tame. Exports exceeded imports, and we had a favorable trade balance. America was fulfilling its promise of becoming the greatest nation and economy in the world, and prosperity resulted.

But we raised a new generation of Americans who were seemingly unhappy with these conditions. We became convinced that our great system of democracy and capitalism was leaving too many people behind while making a few rich, and that it was therefore unfair. Even though I remember that almost everyone was getting much better off than they were before and a great deal of wealth was being accumulated by very many, the perception persisted. So, Lynden Johnson created his Great America Welfare System. I remember that he convinced Congress to allow him to borrow all the money out of the social security trust fund and gave it to the poorest people and others in the country. His welfare system, of course, became permanent and has expanded over time. The policy was certainly well intentioned, but not much attention was paid to the problems it caused. The supply chain in America was already stretched. The increase in demand for products that his giveaways caused was not able to be met and resulted in a very substantial inflation. It is likely everyone my age remembers the inflation of the 1970s.

Cars were increasing ten percent each year, and home mortgage interest rates exceeded ten percent. Labor unions got stronger, and wages followed suit. The price of everything went up substantially. By 1980, manufacturers in this country had already started to outsource the production of goods to foreign countries. In addition to costs of production and labor costs, the government created equal opportunity rules which directed manufacturers to hire according to quotas, which made manufacturing in the United States even more difficult. These changes in government policy made trade so much more important a consideration in the economic policy of this and other countries. Taxes on the supply side were also being raised, and entire companies were considering moving to other countries with lower tax rates. At this point in time, however, supply shortages did not as yet seem to result from these changes in government policy, but substantial inflation and much higher interest rates did.

During the Clinton Administration, however, the United States once again changed trade policy, opening up greater importation of goods from China, India, Canada, and Mexico. Once again, this change was well-intentioned and sold as a program that would benefit all Americans. American corporations would now become much more international and be able to sell products in very large markets not previously available to them. The reverse actually happened. Everything we eat, wear, and use every day began to be made overseas, so that, today, almost all of America's supply chain is overseas. It is my belief that this is the primary cause of our supply chain problem as well as the inflation we are experiencing. America cannot remain at the mercy of foreign countries to supply everything we need and use. We must rebuild supply in the United States. You may remember that, when Barack Obama shut down a substantial portion of oil production in the United States and we became more dependent on foreign oil, the price of a barrel of oil went up to $140 and gasoline was $4.50 a gallon.

Overdependence on supply from other countries is not the only thing that resulted from America's changes in trade policy over the decades. America has had trade deficits because imports have exceeded exports in our country now probably since the 1970s. Allow me to offer a new definition of a trade deficit. A trade deficit is actually a transfer of wealth from the middle class of the United States to the middle class of other countries which have positive trade balances with us. This happens because we are creating jobs and transferring jobs that should be in the United States to foreign countries where all goods are now produced. They are all good paying jobs. Some would argue that we have full employment in the United States and do not need any more jobs. In fact, we need more employees. The truth is exactly the opposite. When I was young, workforce participation, which is the percentage of men of working age working in the country, was 88%. Today, it is less than 62%. That would mean that there are well over 30 million men in the United States that are not working and are not counted in the unemployment ranks. In my opinion, there is substantial evidence that US governments, at all levels, have become too large to be supported by the domestic economy. The governments have become so much larger and the domestic economy, adjusted for inflation, has become smaller. Since the year 2000, the federal government continues to borrow money and give it to people to spend where it is counted in GNP to show growth in demand. If you remove the trillions that the government borrowed in the last twenty years, the true American domestic economy has become a lot smaller. I refer to this as negative government intervention in the US economy, which has been the cause over the years of substantial inflation and stagnation. It would not surprise me to learn that many other Western nations have been doing the same thing for many years.

In my book, I state clearly that the most important aspect of the trade policy of every country is that everything that we use which is possible to be produced in our own country should be produced domestically, regardless of differences in cost of production that might exist. This is important for a number of reasons. To begin with, the best-paying and most important jobs in our country are and will always be in the production of goods here. We have to support our families. We need control over the quality of the products that we use, and it is difficult to control the quality of products made elsewhere. Innovative designs and inventions created here are given over to our foreign suppliers, some of whom, like China specifically, will be future enemies. If military supplies are made overseas, we are not only giving away important trade secrets, but also becoming dependent on other nations for defense. And, in fact, has all this production of everything we use every day overseas not also resulted in the fact that we have unnecessary shortages with resulting inflation? Will there be Christmas for children this year, and will everyone be able to afford it? We MUST bring the production of products we use every day back to the farms and factories here in the United States.

Love,
Lawrence A. Stellato

Love Letter #2:
Religious Fervor

October 22, 2021

Dear America,

We all know that a great deal of friction and a great many wars on planet Earth have been caused by differences in religion. Religions are the source of all ethics and morality, substantially influence our culture and our way of life and are, therefore, of utmost importance in our lives. This subject is discussed briefly in my book, titled *Past, Present, and Future of Planet Earth,* which is available at Barnes and Noble and Amazon in paperback and e-book.

More than likely, in one way or another, practically everyone on planet Earth believes that some dominant power or God is responsible for the existence of the universe, our planet, and all humanity. The universe in which we live is so vast as to be not only beyond our knowledge but perhaps beyond our imagination as well. Maybe our entire solar system is merely one cell of some huge entity. Then the Earth is less than a pebble. Surely, some magnificence is responsible for all of this. The earliest history of intelligent life on our planet came from the history books and stories contained in our religious beliefs.

These are all also the origins of all ethics and morality. It is perhaps unfortunate that so many different cultures developed on our planet, of which religious beliefs were such an important part, that friction and war became our way of life. Wars between Christians and Muslims are legendary and dominate our history books. Differences in beliefs among Roman Catholics were the cause of the formation of many Protestant sects in Christianity, and persecution in Europe and wars in Ireland resulted. Practically all wars in the Middle East are the result of radical Islamic sects which invade and conquer territories for the purpose of gaining control of the government in the regions they conquer. Islam has been spread militarily into many regions of Africa, Asia, and southern Europe also. History tells us that, even in this day and age, there are people who will fight and kill others to spread their culture and religious beliefs. Perhaps, there are also many who will fight to preserve their own culture.

The most important thing about Judaism, Christianity, and Islam is that they all believe in and honor the same God, Who, presumably, created the Earth and all of humanity. All these religions seem to stem from the original Old Testament of the Bible, although only Christians seem to accept the New Testament. Jews and Islamists seem to have created their own additional texts, which appear to enumerate their differences in beliefs. How is it possible that minor differences in understanding the intent of their common God about the things we should believe, the way we should live, and the rules we should follow and live by could be the cause of so much friction, war, and killing? Should not all the members of these religions be attending the same churches while the elders of all of them might be having discussions about the many beliefs they have about which they differ? In fact, many of the things

23

in which we believe can never be proven one way or the other and must be accepted on faith. For example, is Jesus Christ the Son of God? Based on the technology that exists today, He certainly could have been, but it will never be known for sure. There are many other tenets of various religions that may also never be proven. But the real question is: should any of these differences be considered important enough to fight wars or kill each other over? In my opinion, they are not. These are minor differences that we can talk about all day long while we all attend the same church. Religious fervor needs to be modified to a much lower level. Oriental religions appear, in my opinion, to have similar, inconsequential differences.

There is, in fact, a much more important point to make. A study of all of the religions on our planet gives the impression that they all seem to be referring to a god or gods which created and therefore have the right to rule the Earth and all of humanity. This is, of course, due to the fact that at the time all religions developed, the Earth was all that was known of the universe. Today, we know that the Earth is merely a very tiny part of what is likely an incredibly vast universe. I believe there is a God, but He is the Creator of the entire universe and everything in it. Humanity may not be the only living creatures in it. If that is the case, are we not all a part of the same religion? Everyone on planet Earth. Perhaps we should all be attending the same churches and be free to discuss the unimportant differences we have, many of which we may never fully agree upon.

There is another important consideration. Religious beliefs continue to be spread militarily around the world. How can this possibly be right? No one on planet Earth has the right to go into another man's home territory and tell him what he should believe, how he should live, or what his culture should be. If we are to live together in peace on our planet, it appears essential that we all live separately in a place where our religion and culture are accepted and generally practiced. Increased knowledge and understanding of the way things really are will someday, perhaps after we are long gone, bring us all to a more commonly accepted way of life. Until that day comes, globalization is not possible. All people will naturally rebel against forced changes in their culture.

Governments seem to think today that if they just throw everyone of all different religions together in the same place, there will be peace and harmony. That will never be possible as long as people feel so strongly about their beliefs, culture and way of life. Different cultures must remain separated. And religious zealots must stop spreading their beliefs militarily. There is no one correct religion.

Love,
Lawrence A. Stellato

Love Letter #3:
The New World Order

October 26, 2021

Dear America,

The subject of this letter is "The New World Order." Today, I think some people are coming to realize that an effort to globalize the entire planet is taking place and has been for some time. Almost no one understands the direction in which it is headed. Much more needs to be covered in the media about this subject. Certainly, everyone on Earth would like to know what the wealthy and powerful have planned for their future. This subject is covered briefly in my book titled *Past, Present, and Future of Planet Earth,* available at Barnes and Noble and Amazon in paperback and e-book.

I think the first time I heard anything about the New World Order was in the early 1990s. Around that time, the United Nations published an edict which mandated that all world leaders should direct communities to build all housing as flats in apartment buildings along rail lines by which residents could travel to work. There would be much less necessity for automobile travel. This was a shock to me, as it appeared to be an intentional condemnation of the way the American economy was growing. When I was young, I remember that young people in this country were getting married around twenty years old.

By age twenty-five, they had two kids and were able to buy a house in the suburbs. It appeared to me that this was America fulfilling its promise to build the greatest economy ever known to mankind on planet Earth. I was curious as to why the United Nations should discourage this kind of progress for mankind. With further research, I learned that there were many powerful and wealthy people on Earth, as well as in America, who saw the UN as becoming the ruler of the entire world, and that effort had been in existence since shortly after the end of World War II.

Proponents of the New World Order were members of secret societies for many years. Members of wealthy families and attendees at very prestigious universities were invited to join these secret societies and to become aware of this goal of future world domination. The New World Order is no longer a secret. It has come out of the closet, so to speak. Today, you can go to a Barnes and Noble store and buy a book which will tell you about the globalization effort and name many who are members of organizations which support this lofty goal. It is reported in some literature, in fact, that many prominent politicians in the United States are members of such groups, including George Bush Sr. and Jr., Bill and Hillary Clinton, Barack Obama, Joe Biden, and many members of their administrations. It is intended, of course, that the United Nations, under the apparent guidance of many powerful voices, will rule the planet.

At first glance, it would certainly appear that all the people of Earth living in peace under one rule and with the best interests of everyone at heart would most certainly be a worthy goal. After all, everyone who knows anything about world history and geography knows that all societies on planet Earth have been created through conquest and dominated by military strength. From the early Egyptians, Greeks, Spartans, and Roman Empire to the later empires built by England, France, and Spain, and to the efforts of Genghis Khan, Napoleon, Adolph Hitler, the Japanese Empire, and the latest efforts of the USSR, America, and now the expanding influence of China, domination over people has always been attempted. And killing people to achieve it has never been a major impediment. It is truly a sad commentary of world history, but nevertheless true. Unfortunately, we still have no shortage of wealthy and powerful people who believe that they have the solution to the world's problems and that they have the right to tell everyone how to live.

It is my opinion, however, that very substantial evidence exists that the globalization of the Earth is not possible at the present time. We need to examine and understand better how intelligent life on Earth developed and exists now. Vast differences in culture have developed in different areas of the world. In the term culture, I include religion, type of government and social and family life, as well as language, dress and customs. In addition to the domination and takeover of other people's territory, people have been killing each other over religion and the type of government under which they choose to live for many centuries. I see no evidence that people feel less strongly about how they live today.

All ethics and morality that exist on Earth appear to have come from religions. Perhaps many governments would like to stamp out religions and get people to believe that only the government has the right to tell people how to live and what rules to follow. I think they fail to understand how deep religious beliefs are. Jews, all Christians and Islamists all believe in and worship the same God. But the cultures of these religions are vastly different in their way the people live. Jews change the culture of people by infiltration into other societies. But the wars between Muslims and Christians are legendary. And there has been substantial conflict between Catholics and Protestants. Islam has been trying to annihilate Israel and the Jewish religion for centuries. It has apparently become the practice of the New World Order to open borders and infiltrate Christian territories with Muslims, and force people of different faiths to live together, hoping peaceful co-existence will result. Religion is really deep rooted. It is my belief that Islam is being spread militarily to different nations of the world today also. I believe that, in the interest of peaceful co-existence, it is necessary to encourage people of different faiths to remain in places where their faith is accepted and practiced until the day arrives when religious leaders come to understand that the differences in their beliefs are minute and inconsequential and that they should perhaps be all attending the same churches. If history has taught us anything, it is that forced changes in culture will be met with resistance and rebellion.

Throughout history, until several centuries ago, societies were ruled by a king, regent, or family under military control. Lords owned and controlled all the land and means of production and were allowed to control their regions as long as they paid tribute to and supported the king. All of the people were serfs and worked in poverty for the lords. In more recent times, people rebelled against kingdoms and established methods of government in which they voted for their own leaders, hoping to share more equally in the product of their labor. Democracy and communism were born. On planet Earth today, there are still nations ruled by tyrants, but there are also democracies and Communist countries. Very different cultures exist in these very different countries. History has taught us that people will kill each other to maintain their culture or to change the culture and way of life of others. Since the end of World War II, substantial efforts have been made by Communist nations to spread communism to other areas of the world. Wars have been fought in an attempt to contain this effort.

The powers to be, have apparently decreed that the unification and globalization of the planet should take place under the control of the United Nations. It is worthy of note that all ten leaders of the United Nations in its history thus far have been radical socialists and communists. The socialization that is taking place in most of all democratic nations in the world today gives us further indication that the New World Order intends that the planet should come under communist or some sort of Totalitarian control. If it is the intent that the government will maintain control over the people militarily and control ownership of all property and means of production, then it would appear to be nothing more than a return to the status of the kingdoms that existed nearly five hundred years ago, in which the people lived in poverty while the kings and lords prospered. If the common people on planet Earth are to have any means of having a decent living or making any progress toward a better life for themselves through their own effort, then it is essential that democracy and capitalism survive in the New World Order. The Industrial Revolution, which is responsible for all of the inventions that improved the lives of all humanity did not take place in Russia or China. It did not take place in Asia, Africa, Australia or Latin America. It took place in Western Europe and the United States, which was the birthplace of democracy and capitalism. It is my contention that, even today, modern invention of every kind is being born in capitalist and democratic nations because that is where opportunity exists for individual betterment.

We must be careful to preserve every opportunity to continue to better the lives of all intelligent life on our planet. After all, isn't that what we have come to believe that the role of government is in society today? Until such time as we are all in agreement on the type of government in which we should all live, perhaps we should encourage all people to live where their preferred government rule is accepted and exists. We must remember that forced change in culture will normally meet with resistance and rebellion. Through continued education and gradual cultural evolution, a New World Order may take place on its own without being forced.

We may just not be here to see it, but we should leave the idea behind us to suggest a future direction. The world is still just not ready for the globalization which our world leaders feel is ideal and are trying to bring about much more quickly than appears to be possible.

Love,
Lawrence A. Stellato

Love Letter #4:
Global Warming

November 1, 2021

Dear America,

Trillions of dollars are being spent today, and trillions more are planned to be spent to change our way of life because there is evidence that a slight change is taking place in the temperature of our planet and that mankind is the cause. This entire issue of the history of structural changes that have taken on planet Earth, many of which affect climate change, requires media coverage to better inform us all about this subject.

Although intelligent life appeared relatively recently on Earth, the planet has apparently been in existence for eons. From religious records and our own history and geography studies, we have learned that many enormous changes have taken place on our planet during those eons. We have had ice ages. Archeologists tell us that deserts now exist where there were once large bodies of water. I have read that it is likely that some continents that are closer together now were once further apart, and others that were further apart may be closer now. There have been many volcanic eruptions in many different areas of the world. It is legendary how many ships have disappeared in the Bermuda Triangle over the centuries. I recently read a report that states that the Earth may be alternately heating and cooling slightly every eighty years. If the Earth were to rotate around the sun a bit closer or a bit further away every few decades, it would not likely be noticed by scientists. A substantial portion of the known Earth at the time apparently came to be underwater because we are told Noah had to build an ark. Here in the United States, there was a great dust storm in the early 1900s when vast areas of farmland could not be cultivated. I have long wondered if this was a major cause of the stock market collapse in 1929 and the depression of the thirties. It has long been known that our planet has always been undergoing major change, before and after the introduction of intelligent life here, some due to changes in climate and others which were not.

Today, we choose to focus on a minor change in world temperature. Although history tells us that there may be other reasons for this change and we do not seem to know whether it is temporary or permanent, we choose to believe that this change is man-made and caused by the increasing emissions of carbon monoxide into our atmosphere. If climate warming proves to be permanent, it is reasonable to assume that carbon monoxide emissions are at least partially responsible. In my mind, however, many questions remain to be answered.

Once, I was asked a question during a discussion about this topic. If we are removing billions of barrels of oil out of the ground, what are we replacing it with? I have no answer, of course, but it is also true that I have never heard this question asked before: If North America and other sections of our planet were completely covered with ice at one time centuries ago, is it not true then that icebergs have been melting for centuries long before we discovered petroleum and carbon monoxide? Can it be that all of the planets in our solar system have been gradually and

33

very slowly moving closer to the sun since the dawn of time and that gradual warming is common to all of them? Is the sun getting hotter very slowly? What other changes are taking place caused by our dramatically growing population on Earth that may also be a contributor to change?

We need to look at what problems are being caused by this global change in temperature and what solutions are offered. Many of the Earth's governments and prominent leaders will just tell us that the Earth is being destroyed and we will not be able to live here anymore without being very specific. I recently read a report by a group called the "Environmental Defense Fund," which stated some changes they attribute to climate change. They are identified as follows:

• Decreases in global beer and an insecure food supply due to extreme drought and heat resulting in higher food prices.
• Danger and loss of insurance to homes in flood-prone areas.
• Changes in insect control can lead to certain types of deforestation.
• Loss of coral reefs in our oceans.
• Drying up of lakes and rivers.
• Loss of coffee-growing regions.

These are substantial changes. It is interesting that I have never read an article about the changes that occurred when oil production was halted in the United States and ethanol was required to be added to our fuel supply during the Obama administration. Much agricultural land was converted to producing corn for ethanol. Food and gasoline prices escalated substantially, and production of much of our fruit and vegetables went overseas with a corresponding reduction in quality. We still use ethanol today, and production of petroleum at home is again being curtailed under the Biden administration. Prices are rising substantially again. There seems to always be a terrible economic price to pay when the government interferes in the direction of our economy.

What solutions are offered? It seems that we have long since learned to use hydroelectric power, and nuclear energy has been converted to be used for electric power. As solar energy has become more economically practical, we have begun to use solar energy for electric power generation also. We have also begun to use wind for electric power creation. Recently, our lords and masters worldwide seem to have decided that we must immediately convert to total solar energy with enhanced battery storage for the total replacement of gasoline, natural gas, and coal. There is no question that there is a place for solar panels on homes and commercial structures to contribute some of the energy used in those buildings. If we convert all available land for solar energy production, however, to fuel a billion cars and trucks and transportation worldwide, where will we grow food, and how much will it cost? How many thousands of electric plants will we have to add to the grid to store and deliver this power to recharge our vehicles? I believe it is unlikely that solar and wind can possibly deliver all the power that will be needed. In fact, many of the added power plants will actually be forced to use natural gas, coal, and nuclear power. In my mind, there are questions as to whether the emissions from natural gas and coal are much better for the environment than the carbon monoxide that we are getting now. It is also worthy of note that nuclear power, while it produces cleaner energy, also produces nuclear waste material that is extremely dangerous and must be stored in the Earth's crust. Nuclear waste can remain deadly to human life for hundreds of years.

I recently wrote a book called *Past, Present, and Future of Planet Earth.* In this text, I mention that it is my contention that government interference in a productive beneficial economy always seems to have devastating effects on the lives of the people it serves. It certainly appears that conversion to as much solar and wind power as is practical would be beneficial. But the economy has already started to do that on its own without help, to the extent that it is practical. Petroleum use will gradually decrease and should not be stopped until it is no longer needed. The population of planet Earth has been throwing garbage in the oceans and causing damage to our air and water forever, and the population keeps increasing. Perhaps the trillions we are planning to spend on the conversion of our energy sources would be better spent trying to clean up after ourselves as much as possible. It is noteworthy that the United States and Europe, who have done so much to clean up their own air and water, are asked to deliver so much to the solution while the major polluters of the world, like Russia, China, India, and other nations, are given a pass to continue to pollute the environment in the near term. Some additional common sense needs to be added to worldwide energy policy.

Love,
Lawrence A. Stellato

Love Letter #5:
Will Interest Rates Rise?

November 26, 2021

Dear America,

We have been and are still experiencing a great deal of inflation recently in the prices we pay for goods and services. Just about every economist and security analyst in the country is asking not just when but how high will interest rates go as a result. I believe there are economic factors that influence rates that are not being properly discussed and should be. Perhaps this will shed some additional light on the subject.

Interest rates are the cost of capital. It is the price we pay for borrowed money. In a normal economy, interest rates would rise if capital is in short supply, and rates would fall if capital was more than adequate. A normal economy, however, assumes that all products and services consumed in our country are made here and that the government does not interfere in normal economic activity. Since neither of these things has been the case in this country since the 1970s, looking back on what happened in the past may not be representative of what will happen this time. Looking back to the past to make predictions is still the method used by all economists and analysts.

What has changed? Actually, the government has

changed everything in our economy that affects the level of interest rates. The most significant factor is the change that has occurred on the supply side. Almost nothing is made in the United States any more. Why would anyone need to borrow money to make products in this country anymore? There is surely a reduction in demand for capital to produce goods. In the meantime, any interruption in the supply chain resulting from a lack of capability to produce goods in our supplier countries or in the transportation capability to get the goods to us when needed will increase the costs consumers pay and result in inflation here at home. This is, of course, exactly what we are experiencing right now. These facts would tend to keep interest rates low at a time when we expect them to rise.

Unfortunately, this is not all that the government has changed. Government is borrowing way more than ever before, which will increase the need for borrowed money and tend to raise rates eventually. In addition, the government has been increasing welfare programs, giving people money to spend. This increases demand for products which we cannot right now get from overseas, and this will also have a substantial impact on increasing inflation. The government is also in the mood to substantially increase taxes. The intent appears to be that the largest impact will be on the wealthy, where normally supply-side capital is likely to be created. Reductions in capital or labor on the supply side also normally will tend to increase inflation.

Will interest rates rise? There are two dangers. If inflation continues unabated, as is currently happening, pressure will mount on the Federal Reserve Bank to raise interest rates to combat inflation. Pressure is already mounting. If the Fed does raise interest rates, it will cause a recession, as it has done so many times in the past. It is also true that if the government continues to borrow so much money as it has been doing since 2000 and raise taxes, especially on the wealthy, as it is so fond of doing, it will reduce the capability of wealthy individuals to buy the new Treasury bonds being issued, and this will also put upward pressure on interest rates.

Generally speaking, of course, low interest rates and balanced supply and demand, which tend to keep inflation under control, are extremely beneficial to the health of our economy. What then should be the solution to the out-of-balance conditions the government is imposing upon the economy that will help us return to a more healthy economic balance? The most important thing we have to do, of course, is to bring the supply chain back to America. This will increase our need for capital here in the United States, but it will also reduce the need for welfare programs by bringing jobs back, which we have been shipping to overseas countries since the 1970s. It will likely also increase tax revenue for the government and reduce its need to borrow.

The second important thing we have to accomplish is to reduce the size of all government activity in the country. It is my opinion that government at all levels has grown way too large to be supported by the private economy of the country. As a result, governments at all levels continue to borrow more and more to support their existence and programs because economic activity cannot generate enough tax money to support them. Eventually, if perpetuated, this has to result in economic failure. We must reduce the size of governments and reduce government borrowing.

The United States, as well as so many other countries, have

gone a very long way down the road in the wrong direction. It will take a long time to get back on the road to economic balance. But it is the proper way forward. I am not alone in predicting that, if we continue on our present path, economic destruction lies ahead. Recently, the inflation we are experiencing appears to be spreading worldwide. Under the circumstances, it appears more and more likely that other nations will also be pressured to increase interest rates, which is the preferred method of fighting inflation. We could be headed for a worldwide recession. Each nation must learn to gain greater control over their own supply side to control inflation within their own country, so that raising interest rates will not be necessary to bring it back under control.

Love,
Lawrence A. Stellato

Love Letter #6:
Types of Government

December 11, 2021

Dear America,

The title of this letter is "Types of Government." It occurs to me that, within the general public, there is a lack of understanding about government and how important it is to understand the impact that the government that rules us has on our daily lives. This letter may have an educational impact on the lives of all Americans.

During the long history of intelligent life on planet Earth, there have been a number of cultural issues that humans consider so important that they have been the reason for friction and war for eons. There have been battles for control of land masses, religious differences, different types of society, different types of government, different types of economies, and different types of social cultures. More recently, changes in trade relations have caused such dramatic changes in lifestyle in different countries that trade may also become another cause of conflict. In the last several centuries, the type of government has become one of the most important. Regardless of what we choose to call a government, it occurs to me that all forms of government will fall under three general types.

We all know that, originally, planet Earth contained no

intelligent life. Science tells us that the beginnings of humanity were indeed humble. We all came from animals after all and before the origin of religious beliefs, there were no rules of law, ethics, or morality. All of the earliest societies lived by the laws of the jungle. We were animals after all. The strongest, or alpha male, ruled, protected, and provided for the tribe, making up the rules as he went along. So the earliest societies were all kingdoms. How can we call this type of society anything but a kingdom? Although experiments were done at times during history with having a senate to represent the common people, this type of society (kingdoms) has survived as the only type of government on planet Earth until modern times. Greek, Spartan, and Roman societies, for example, briefly had Senates. As populations expanded, kings eventually had to maintain large armies to control their populations. But down through the entire history of our planet, people who controlled all societies on our planet and were supported by wealthy property owners ruled over the people in their territories as kings and made all the rules. So kingdoms were the first, original, and only type of society on planet Earth for eons.

In my first book, *Past, Present, and Future of Planet Earth*, I speculate that three original races of humans, yellow, white, and black, which later mixed, were created in three different locations of the planet. In the areas occupied by the white race, primarily in Western Europe, people revolted against the rule of their kings and began two different types of government in which, for the very first time in the history of our planet, people would have some say in who their rulers should be. Democracy was born in Europe, and communism was born in Russia. Although they are very different kinds of governments, neither qualifies as a kingdom. I am not an expert in modern history, but it makes sense to me that democracy came first. In a democracy, the people's representatives make the laws that we live by, we elect the executive branch that enforces the laws and a judicial branch maintains fairness and justice in the system. Democracy has spread into many countries and, although convoluted everywhere with socialism and too much control exercised by the executive branch in many places, still survives in many countries. Democracy permits the ownership of capital and property by the people, not just the government and the wealthy and, if honest elections can be maintained, the majority of the people control who is in the government.

Communism began in Russia after a very bloody revolution during which the regents were very reluctant to give up control. Theoretically, in communism, the people elect their leaders, to whom they give the complete right to control all property and capital for the benefit of the people, who are all to be treated equally. Communism has spread into many countries also. If the leaders of Communist governments and those who control all of the property and capital in those countries all truly lived in the same conditions as those that they govern, we would have true communism. But just like democracy, communism is surely convoluted. Government leaders and those that control the assets surely live a better life than those they govern.

Planet Earth, it seems, will never have a shortage of people who feel they are better than everyone else and have the right to rule and tell everyone else how to live. Mark Zuckerberg, who is actually Mark Greenberg, has been quoted as saying that the common people are all animals who need to be controlled. George Soros gives hundreds of millions of dollars each year to help elect officials who will work in various countries to help communize the planet. The New World Order works constantly to promote the control of all the nations of the Earth under the United Nations. I have read that the New World Order, in addition to George Soros, includes many wealthy and powerful people who govern other countries but also includes George

43

Bush Sr. and Jr., the Clintons, the Obamas, Biden and others. I have read that all ten of the leaders of the United Nations until today have all been radical socialists or communists. It seems that, if today's world leaders get their way, we will all be living under communism down the road.

There are still three types of governments on planet Earth. Many nations are still ruled by tyrants who have the power of a king over their people and maintain military control. Democratic and Communist governments, although not in their original intended form, exist in many countries. If history has taught us anything, it has taught us that we the people, will be fighting against people trying to enslave us until the end of time. Certainly, kings and tyrants enslave their people. In communism, how can you better your life if it is against the law for you to accumulate any wealth or property? It occurs to me that the most important thing that the common people have won over time in revolt is the capability to improve their lives. If we are to live under totalitarianism, it must include capitalism. In my opinion, capitalism is the very reason for all the improvements that have taken place in society worldwide in the last two centuries. Why would anybody create anything to improve the lives of everyone if there is no incentive to do so? In my lifetime, I have watched so many of the freedoms achieved by so many gradually disappearing in so many countries. Powerful forces are making it happen. It is my opinion that the world will stagnate and freedom and betterment for the lives of the common people will disappear if we allow democracy and capitalism to disappear from planet Earth.

Eventual global guidance by the United Nations over all of the nations on the planet may not be ultimately a bad idea. It would be a wonderful thing to have worldwide peace and harmony. But totalitarianism will no longer be tolerated ultimately by everyone in this modern world. We still have differences in religion and culture over which we kill each other. We still have differences in types of government, over which we continue to kill each other. We still have tyrants who will not submit to the rule of the United Nations. Fortunately, it is also my belief that we still have some leaders and wealthy people who believe that we must preserve the rights and freedoms of the common people that were won by revolution centuries ago, which include the right to elect their government and own property and capital. We also have history, which tells us that people will rebel against those who would change their religious beliefs or culture or exercise totalitarian control over their lives. A United Nations which accepts and attempts to guide the planet for the betterment of all might be beneficial. A United Nations which is dedicated to total control is more likely to contribute to an increase in friction and war than it would be to contribute to a peaceful planet.

Love,
Lawrence A. Stellato

Love Letter #7:
Illusion of American Prosperity

December 30, 2021

Dear America,

The title of this letter is "Illusion of American Prosperity." It seems to me that the economy of the United States is reported as being sound and growing, but my own experience and knowledge tell me that it may not be. This letter may inspire more Americans to think more intuitively about government interference in the economy and what it reports to us about financial conditions.

Despite brief interludes of recession, our government reports to us that our economy is sound and growing and has always been. I was born in 1939, grew up in the 1950s and studied in the 1950s and 1960s. I consider myself to have been an observer and student of the economy, government and changes in social structure of the United States for about the last sixty years. There are too many times that I read government reports about financial conditions so important to our lives which raise questions in my mind. I do remember that after World War II, in the late 1940s and 1950s, the economy of the United States was extremely healthy. The entire world wanted to buy American-made products; everyone was employed in good jobs and the lives of all young people were continually growing financially healthier. It is my belief, however, that what I have witnessed in my

46

lifetime is a continual decline in the economy of our country since the 1960s. If 120 million people were employed when the population was 180 million and 140 million are employed now when the population is 330 million, how could everyone be doing well? How could we have full employment, as is being reported? I believe that at least 190 million people would have to be employed to have comparable full employment. If we produced and sold 17 million vehicles in the United States when the population was 180 million and we barely sell the same amount today, of which the parts are all made overseas, to a much larger population, how is this economic growth? I think everyone knows today that practically nothing is manufactured in our country any more. In fact, we probably produce much less of what we eat also. The dramatic inflation of the 1970s, which, I believe, was caused by government interference in the economy and coupled by the highest taxes on corporations in the world, created a massive flow of jobs out of our country and into other nations. After 1980, the outflow of jobs was temporarily suspended by Reaganomics and tax reductions. But, again in the Clinton era, new trade agreements that opened new trade with other countries began a new shift of millions more jobs to China, India, Mexico, Canada and other countries. These massive transfers of jobs to overseas countries, primarily caused by our own government interfering in the economy, represents a huge transfer of wealth from the middle class of the United States to the middle classes of other countries. That loss can be measured by the incredible trade deficits we have incurred, which began in the 1970s. Initial trade deficits may have been counted in the billions, but today's trade deficits have been one trillion dollars each year for the last several years. These deficits do not represent losses to the wealthy in our country who are getting

47

wealthier. They are losses to our working middle class.

If these reductions in economic activity have truly taken place here, how can it be, then, that the government continually reports to us increases in gross national product (GNP)? Well, there is, of course, inflation. If the numbers were not properly adjusted for inflation, we could be reporting imaginary growth. I remember that I paid $2866 for my first new car which was a 1966 Chevrolet Impala. That same car today would cost in excess of $40,000, which is an increase of nearly 10% compounded annually since 1966. Everything we drive, eat, and use today has escalated in price at a similar rate since that time. It is my belief that, if we counted true economic activity in items produced instead of dollars, we would see that true economic activity is less today than it was many years ago.

We also need to look carefully at how we count the gross national product. Is what we are counting all economic activity originated in and flowing through our private economy? Although taxes collected by the government is money that has been diverted from the private economy and may be used for purposes other than intended by industry or consumers, tax money, in my opinion, is part of gross national product. However, since at least the year 2000, it seems to have become traditional for us to raise the country's debt ceiling and allow the government to borrow more and more money which is then used to increase the size of government and given to people in welfare spending. Money borrowed by corporations to produce goods is economic activity and stimulates the economy. Borrowing by the government is a different animal. It is printed by the government and not created by the private economy. Why would a supplier increase production capacity to provide goods paid for by borrowed government money. Theoretically, the government would not borrow again every year to require the same supply. Money printed by the government should not be counted in the gross national product. It is also inflationary because it would not be accompanied by an increase in supply of products to purchase. On the other hand, overproduction of products by the supply side of the economy would result in deflation. It is likely that our government has borrowed about $25 trillion since the year 2000. I think most Americans know that government debt has grown today to about $27 trillion. If we were to reduce the reported gross national product numbers by the amount borrowed each year and added to the economy by government, I believe that the result would be a reduction in each year of gross national product. That would mean that the true private economy would have been in depression since 2000. I also believe that, if we could more accurately adjust for inflation, the numbers would be even worse. Although there was some snap back in the 1980s and 1990s, I believe we could look at what happened in the 1970s in the same way. The only difference appears to me to be that Lynden Johnson borrowed the money he used to create the welfare system from social security and did not increase the national debt or require debt ceiling increases.

It is my contention that it is one of any government's most important jobs to report economic activity accurately to its citizens. It is even more important that the purpose of government should be to promote economic activity in the best interests of its citizens. We have to improve the way we report jobs and economic activity. But we should also be insistent that our government's economic policies be in the best interests of American citizens. I am implying that the United States and other countries may be distorting reporting deliberately to justify transferring wealth from formerly wealthier countries to what used to be poorer nations. But each nation has the obligation to support the economic activity in its own country so that it is in the best interests of its own citizens. The U.S. government transferred millions and millions of jobs from our country to foreign nations in the 1970s and again in the early 2000s, deliberately transferring middle-class wealth from the United States to the middle-class citizens of other nations. And it reports to us a healthy labor market, which is greatly reduced from many years ago and perhaps not as healthy as is reported.

Love,
Lawrence A. Stellato

Love Letter #8:
Equality and Equality of Opportunity

February 8, 2022

Dear America,

You cannot listen to a radio or TV broadcast or read a newspaper today without seeing constant discussion of equality. This is not limited to racial inequality but also has been extended to include gender inequality and non-citizens, as well as prejudice related to sexual preference, and certainly pertains to the financial and social status of the individuals against whom we are prejudiced. This has become so widespread that it seems that the government today, in its own policies, insists that we, in our own lives, give preference to everyone except white European American male citizens of the United States who are Christians. The people in this group have seemingly become a very small minority compared to all the people we believe they are prejudiced against.

The government would like us to believe that this prejudice is systemic—in other words, built into our American way of life. What we are being told is that, in order to achieve equality, we must give special preference to almost everyone in all levels of education, jobs, government contracts, and almost everything else in life to everyone except white male citizens. Even illegal aliens receive free healthcare, which is not available to citizens. It seems that our own government would like us to believe that our constitution and our American way of life is the ultimate cause of all this injustice.

Are we right about any of this? Of course not. First of all, the billionaires and government officials who would impose these restrictions on the population will not give up their own priority status and wealth to live like the rest of us. We are also long past the time when we can claim that any group of individuals has not achieved in the United States. There are millionaires and even billionaires of every color. Jews have high-ranking positions in education, law, government and industry and have become wealthy. Illegal aliens have settled here and succeeded in business and accumulated wealth. There is a multitude of evidence telling us that systemic prejudice does not exist in this country. All we have telling us to believe it is our own government and the media. Our government appears to be using this dialogue to achieve more control over the population, and the media appears to be complicit.

Is equality even the issue? I do not believe that the goal of our forefathers when they created this country was to achieve equality for all. Equality for all is communism and that was not their goal. I believe that their goal was equality of opportunity. Because equality of opportunity existed in Western Europe and the United States, capitalism had the opportunity to begin here. All other governments worldwide that existed at the time were either kingdoms or communists. Capitalism, which is the very foundation of all the inventions which created our comfortable living, did not begin in China or the Oriental world. It did not begin in Africa or Latin America. It did not begin in the Communist countries. It was the principle of equal opportunity for all citizens which made capitalism possible. It was the idea that anybody could create something that would improve the lives of others, obtain capital to produce and distribute it, and profit from this venture that made capitalism possible. This opportunity only existed in Western Europe and the United States.

I believe that equality of opportunity is the proper goal. We need to ask ourselves if achieving true equality for all in communism would eliminate the capability for any progress for mankind on planet Earth by the elimination of capitalism from our way of life.

Love,
Lawrence A. Stellato

Love Letter #9:
Is Government Too Big?

February 12, 2022

Dear America,

We are so busy living our lives every day that it is likely never or only on a very rare occasion that we give much thought to our government, and most of those thoughts will be around election time. We elect who we think is best and assume that they will run the country in our best interest. We could not be more wrong. First of all, it used to be that only influence of elections by people like George Soros, who gives hundreds of millions to anti-American candidates who would change our way of life was a problem. Now in my opinion, possibly as far back as the year 2000, we have to wonder if even our national elections were stolen as well by the introduction of phony manufactured votes and to what extent this may be happening. There are, it seems, a great many wealthy and very powerful people in the United States and outside who are very determined to change our way of life, not only in this country but on all of planet Earth.

Is our government actually run by elected officials? Most of it is not. We do not, for example, elect the heads of the CIA, FBI, or IRS. In fact, I cannot tell you who they report to. Maybe they are allowed to do what they want and report to no one. But I read an article recently written by a former Facebook insider who stated that the head of the CIA and the head of Harvard University at the time worked with Mark Zuckerberg, formerly Mark Greenberg, to create Facebook as an online outlet which would be addictive to likely billions of people and through which the government could control what we read and influence what we think. In the same article, Mark Zuckerberg was quoted as saying that the common people are animals which should be kept in cages. Presumably, he includes his own Facebook users in that category. There have been many stories in recent years, although you will not read about them in the mainstream media, that FBI agents have been involved in helping to incite the riots we do not read about taking place in many cities around the country, like Seattle and Portland. It is also said that it was FBI agents who opened the Capitol doors and invited in Trump supporters who were demonstrating peacefully on January 6, 2001, so that they could arrest as many as possible and call them violent protestors. You can read *The Deep State* by Alex Newman to learn how many departments of our government are actually run by individuals who are controlled by leaders of the New World Order and are totally devoted to destroying personal individual freedoms, democracy and capitalism.

There have been stories that the IRS deliberately targeted conservative people, and both the IRS and FBI have targeted and raided the homes of people who opposed government policy in the media. We also do not elect the Chairman of the Federal Reserve Bank, who has more control over our economic system than anyone else in government. I do believe that these things have happened and will continue to happen because the government has become way too large and runs counter to its original intention. The CIA, FBI, IRS, Federal Reserve Bank, and even the Department of Equal Opportunity are all not used today for the purpose for which they were intended. They are all being used today to further the intention of our government to gain more and more control over our personal lives and wealth and to undermine our freedom and independence.

Size of government, certainly to some extent, has to be determined by the role that our government is intended to play in our society. Kingdoms still exist on planet Earth. The role of government in a kingdom or in a Communist country would certainly be different than what it was intended to be by our forefathers, who created our republic to support our democratic way of life and permit capitalism to develop and grow here and improve the lives of everyone on planet Earth. In my opinion, the role of government is to determine the needs of the people and the resources we have available to meet those needs, and then to create the commercial and economic system necessary to provide those needs for its people. The resources we do not have we must trade to get. No other trade should be encouraged unless it is in the best interest of the people of this country. In the last twenty odd years, our government has agreed to trade pacts which have sent many millions of the best American jobs to foreign countries. Everyone knows that nothing we use and practically nothing that we eat is produced or grown in this country any more. The loss of those jobs has been devastating to our economy. This is important to this discussion because the most important determinant of the size of our government has to be the size of our economy.

Government does not have its own money just because it is the government. And it certainly should not be printing as much money as it wants or feels it needs. Government borrowing money has an incredible effect on the economy and is the primary cause of the practically runaway inflations we had in the 1970s and we are experiencing again today. Any economist will tell you that such runaway inflation has the capability to entirely destroy our economy. Most economists believe that raising interest rates by the Federal Reserve Bank can cure this abnormality. I believe that is not true. Inflation is caused by an imbalance of supply and demand in our economy. Raising interest rates could very well reduce both demand and supply and cause a recession. The answer to inflation must include reducing demand and increasing supply at the same time. To increase supply, which is the most important element of this formula, we must reduce taxes on business and re encourage the supply chain to come back to the United States. To reduce demand, we must reduce the capability of our government to borrow money and give it to people to spend at a time when we have no capability to produce the goods needed here in this country and have lost control over our supply chain anyway. Everything we need comes from overseas. So while the government has been growing ever larger over the last fifty or more years, inflation aside, our economy has grown much smaller as more and more jobs have been sent overseas.

We need to consider that every dollar that a government pays to its own employees or to its retired employees or uses to fund the military to protect us has to be generated by our private economy and taken by the government as taxes. It would make sense for the government to borrow money to build infrastructure to support our economy, as long as it eventually gets paid back so that it is later available again to rebuild or improve infrastructure. Our government has been fond of giving money away to foreign countries and conducting wars for many years, as well as creating many other programs which are very costly and not necessarily beneficial for Americans. It may have been arguable in earlier years that perhaps these programs were affordable, but that is certainly not true today. The United States is broke, thirty trillion dollars in debt, and getting broker every day. There is no question that we cannot afford what our government is spending today. I think that the first year of the Biden administration resulted in about $3 trillion in spending over tax income, creating additional borrowing. During the Obama administration, which never even created a budget, the government overspent tax income by about $1.5 trillion every year, despite the largest tax increases in the history of our country. Higher taxes and cost of living by inflation also encourages additional jobs moving overseas to other countries, and will further destroy our economy. Taxes in the United States are certainly high enough to support the minimal economy we have left in this country. The government likely takes in about $3.5 trillion in taxes annually. That is only at the federal level. There are many other jurisdictions that tax us depending on where we live. And they all also borrow. There should never be a need for any government in this great country to borrow any money that will never be paid back and likely will probably just be used to create new programs and make the government larger.

I am suggesting a new economic principle which was not taught when I went to college and likely has never been taught at all. We need to establish a rule for how large the total government in the United States can be as measured by a percentage of the economy, and this should never be exceeded. Borrowing can never be paid for by higher taxes, and no borrowing should ever be allowed that is not scheduled for payback over time so that it will become available again for future needs. Our government would have us believe that when it borrows money and gives it away or spends it, it is stimulating the economy. Nothing could be further from the truth. Borrowed money given by the government to people to spend helps the people you give it to temporarily, but it provides no incentive to the supply side to increase production, especially since nothing is produced here and we have lost control over our supply chain anyway. We all know it also increases inflation. When government spends tax dollars, it does divert the money which would otherwise be used in the economy for different purposes, but it is at least spending money that was produced in the private economy and not created by borrowing.

It is true that sixty or seventy years ago, when I was young, there were only 180 million people in the United States. Today, there are about 330 million. Government does have to be larger to support a larger population. The problem is that our economy is not larger than it was fifty or sixty years ago. The numbers of dollars are larger, but inflation has to be excluded. We are not producing or growing more things in this country now than we were then. Especially not as it relates to population growth. That is why we have an economy that is 70% retail. The fact that our economy is only 30% non-retail tells us by definition that demand will always exceed supply as it relates to our domestic economy and we will always be on the verge of economic destruction from inflation and dependent on other parts of the world for the things we need.

It is perfectly obvious that we do not have enough energy which is contributing substantially to inflation at the present time when everyone knows we have it here but refuse to produce it. It may have been a bit idiotic to deliberately ship all our jobs overseas but not build new ports to bring additional supplies in from foreign countries. We developed new industries dependent on chips but never built new plants here to develop and build our own chips. Government in the United States has very definitely grown too large, lost its purpose and is contributing in so many ways to the total destruction of our once great economic system. Growth in size of government and government borrowing is not limited only to the United States. I believe that there is likely not one government left on planet Earth which has not grown so large that it can no longer be paid for by its local economy. In the United States, I have read that, for many years now, spending by the federal government alone exceeds 25% of the total gross national product. If we add spending by all of the states and municipalities, only God knows how high the number actually is. In my opinion, spending by governments at all levels is dramatically too high and causing economic destruction if it exceeds 20% of the gross national product of the nation. Even at that level, it challenges my imagination to understand how the local economy can support it.

What changes are required in our country and all others in order for us to be able to say that we all have conservative governments which espouse economic principles that have the best interest of their citizens at heart? Total taxes cannot exceed 20% of the gross national product of the country. There is no reason why any government needs more than that level of spending to support itself and the programs the people can afford. No borrowing of any kind should be permitted for money to be used for the daily activities of the government. In other words, no deficit spending. A plan should be available for paying back all government spending on infrastructure so that the borrowing will be available again later for rebuilding or additional infrastructure. In our democratic society, the government should never be allowed to own any business or private capital. Greater limits need to be placed on the Federal Reserve Banks. These banks were created specifically for the purpose of assisting the economy in times of need. They have become controllers of certain aspects of our economies, and their activities substantially exceed their original intention. Federal Reserve Banks should not buy government bonds or bonds of private companies, thereby lending money to the government or acquiring ownership of capital. If government wrongfully borrows money to give to people to spend for which supply is not available and causes inflation by doing so, the Federal Reserve Bank should not raise interest rates in an attempt to correct the problem. Raising the interest rates may cause reduction in both supply and demand, as far as we know, and cause recession which does normally occur at these times. Rebalancing supply with demand is the correct answer which is caused by lowering taxes on business and making more capital available at a lower cost to suppliers in our own domestic economy so that they can rebuild supply to meet the increased demand here at home where it is dependable.

Conservative economics has been dead not only in our own country but worldwide for so long that I do not know if we can ever recover from the damage. We are so fond today of talking about higher taxes on the wealthy. What will happen if government borrowing reaches the point where the wealthy no longer have the capital to buy the debt? If governments default, will all working people who have retirement accounts holding 40% of their assets in government bonds lose almost half of their retirement funds? I am not alone in predicting substantial negative outcomes of present government policies. Most economists and financial analysts know of these dangers. Gold and silver used to be the inflation hedge that people would invest in to avoid losses in times like these. Unfortunately, a great many people have gone to crypto currency assets instead. This may also prove to be a mistake. After the fall of the Roman Empire, the world faced 400 years of the Dark Ages. Our history tells us this. I continue to hope that reality will return to our leadership. If it does not, I fear that planet Earth will be faced with the possibility of another 400 years of future self-inflicted Dark Ages.

Love,
Lawrence A. Stellato

Love Letter #10:
Sovereign Debt

March 6, 2022

Dear America,

It mystifies me to watch investment portfolio managers run to hide investment money in government bonds when they see the stock market in decline. Surely, the balance sheets of most corporations, even some with too much debt, are in better shape than the balance sheets of most governments. Every year, it occurs to me that government bonds become harder and harder to pay back, and interest rates remain unrealistically low.

How deeply in debt are governments on planet Earth? I recently did some research to try to better understand just how bad the problem is. Has the problem of sovereign debt been getting worse? The website **Nationsonline.org** only shows the amount of debt of individual nations up to 2012, along with the percent of gross national product it represents in each nation. Following is a partial list:

Country	Debt	% of GPN
Austria	$352 billion	72%
Belgium	$413 billion	99%
Canada	$1.4 trillion	85%
France	$2.2 trillion	86%

Germany	**$3.1 trillion**	**82%**
Greece	**$294 billion**	**161%**
Ireland	**$182 billion**	**105%**
Japan	**$4.4 trillion**	**230%**
United States	**$15.1 trillion**	**103%**

These are all Western nations with large, prosperous economies, which, if they were to fall into decline, would cause a "Dark Ages" worse than what the planet suffered through after the collapse of the Roman Empire. I believe I read that, in recent years, Greece, Italy, and Portugal were bailed out by the European Union.

How much worse has it gotten since 2012? All of these nations and many others have accumulated much more debt, and their debt is higher in relation to GNP. Most Americans know today that American debt now exceeds $30 trillion which represents about 135% of our Gross National Product. It is likely that this number does not even include the money the government owes to the social security system and possibly the Medicare system also. At $30 trillion, the national debt of the United States represents almost $90,000 for each person in our population of 334 million.

What has caused the United States and other countries to become so deep in debt? What is the likelihood that the U.S. or any of the other Western countries will begin to reduce their debt burdens any time soon? It is not just unlikely. It is probably impossible. While the economy of the U.S. and its Gross National Product appear higher today than they did fifty to seventy years ago due to inflation in the numbers, we have been exporting practically all of our production and jobs to overseas countries since the 1970s. The economy of the U.S. is actually much smaller than it was many years ago. The percentage of the population that had a job in the 1960s was about two-thirds. Today, it is less than half. Labor force participation is way down. In the meantime, the government has grown much larger, not only in number of workers, but in payroll and purpose also. If the size and cost of the government has grown so large that it can no longer be supported by taxation from the local economy, how will the government ever be able to stop borrowing? The budget of the present administration is about $3 trillion more than the taxes to be collected. In addition, the administration has already gotten approval for an additional $2 trillion in additional spending and wants $5 trillion more. This is in addition to the $6 trillion that was borrowed to fight the pandemic. Not only the United States but also most other Western nations have embarked on a policy in which borrowing no longer matters to them and it appears to me that none of them ever have any intention of ever paying any of it back.

In my first book, called *Past, Present, and Future of Planet Earth*, I introduce several new economic principles that, I believe, are needed to save our planet from economic calamity. The first relates to the size of government. A government can never be allowed to increase to a size which cannot be supported by its local economy. Soon, you are using tax money to pay the interest on the debt and there is no money left to provide for the needs of the people. We are even borrowing to pay government employees and the retirements of former government employees.

My book also brings up a new definition for trade deficits. A trade deficit is the transfer of wealth from the middle class of our country to the middle classes of other countries who have positive trade balances with us. The United States has had substantial trade deficits since the 1970s, and they have gotten much worse over the years and total many trillions of dollars. What it means is that we have sent all of our best manufacturing and other types of jobs to overseas countries at the expense of our own middle-class workers. In the meantime, the government keeps growing in size and cost.

How long will countries be able to continue to borrow more and more to support their activities and avoid default on their debt? There are a number of changes taking place today which will tend to bring the planet back to reality. Consider the following:

• Communist and socialized economies have continued to make the rich richer. Sentiment is growing to tax the rich at higher rates. If the rich have less money, they will have less to invest in government bonds.

• Federal Reserve banks worldwide have flooded local economies with capital. Governments have stepped in to borrow a great deal of the available extra capital with resulting inflation. Now, inflation has caused the Federal Reserve banks to embark on a policy of reducing available capital and raising interest rates to fight inflation. This will result in substantially less capital available for purchase of government debt.

• Federal Reserve policy and reduced government spending will result in a recession, at which time less money is available for government borrowing.

• For many years, our government seems to support the export of jobs overseas. No change in this policy seems likely. We need to bring jobs back to America to increase our domestic economy and regain control over our supply chain to help reduce the extent of inflation. Our domestic economy needs to grow again to help support our overinflated government.

• Government must be reduced in size, which will result in less necessity to borrow and increase debt.

- Government debt should only be justified to fund infrastructure. Even then, a plan should be made for how to pay it back so that it will become available again to rebuild infrastructure or create new infrastructure as needed.

It is not a question of if, but when will governments be forced to default on their debt because of lack of availability of additional borrowing capability. Who will suffer? Where will the government get the money to continue to support the welfare programs that it borrows to support now? If you are working and have a 401K, it likely is 40% invested in various government bond programs. Default will hurt you. It is normally the wealthy who provide most of the capital for rebuilding our domestic economy that provides jobs for Americans. We have to start diverting more capital away from government and into the domestic economy.

We have not lost the battle for saving the planet yet, but we are a long way down the road to economic devastation. The United States and all of the Western nations where capitalism still has a foothold must adopt conservative economic principles and rebuild their local economies instead of borrowing to prop up failing economies which they are doing today. We need to think about the consequences. It is my belief and that of many others that the default of worldwide government debt will result in worldwide economic collapse and many years of Dark Ages. No country will survive it.

Love,
Lawrence A. Stellato

Love Letter #11:
Are We Still Democrats or Republicans?

April 1, 2022

Dear America,

Although it may not be widely understood by voters, the terms democrat and republican were intended to identify a substantial difference in thinking about how our country should be managed. The United States was set up by our forefathers to be a republic of states loosely managed by a federal government. A democracy was intended to be a government with more authority over the states. The difference would indicate the level of federal control we wanted our federal government to have. Few people in our time are affiliated with either party for that reason.

When I was young, I saw the Democratic Party as tending to increase the size of government and increasing taxes. The Republican Party was more moderate and the Conservative Party favored lower taxes and a smaller federal government. I was a Conservative until that party disappeared, and then became a Republican. Although I could never understand why anyone would vote for higher taxes and more government control over our lives, it is my opinion that Democrats have been in charge of our government for most of my lifetime.

It later became common to some extent to refer to politicians as Liberals or Conservatives. As I understood it, Liberals would refer to politicians who preferred a larger role for the federal government which would, of course, require higher taxes, and who would like to redistribute as much wealth as possible among the population, which would create the illusion that government was giving free things to certain groups of people. Nothing is free, of course, but they are taking it from one group to give it to another or borrowing money to give it away. Conservatives are rarer and would tend to object to such a redistribution of wealth. I have always tended to be a conservative in this regard, although I am a great believer in charity playing a very important role in the redistribution of wealth. If you have extra and you see people in need, you should be willing to share what you can. But I have always believed that should be left to the people to decide and the power to decide who gets such benefits does not belong in the hands of the government.

Up until recent times, we have actually been voting on how much power our own government should have over American citizens and what our own tax levels and social structure should be. Regardless of why we think we have been Republican or Democrat or Liberal or Conservative, this is what we have been actually voting for. In my lifetime, I believe that our government in the United States of America has practically always been controlled by Democrats and Liberals and has therefore continually grown immensely in size, and there cannot be much question about how high tax structures are worldwide as well as in our own country. In my first book, entitled *Past, Present, and Future of Planet Earth*, I endeavor to create a new conservative economic principle which states that no government should ever grow so large that it can no longer be supported by its local economy. It is my contention that there is no country left on planet Earth in which the government has not outgrown the capability of its local economy to support it. And that is certainly true of the United States also. As evidence of this fact, just look at the level of sovereign debt that exists worldwide. I'm sure that no country would ever be capable of paying back any of its debt. In fact, it is not likely that any of them ever intend to pay any of it back. And they all intend to continue to borrow more. So, whether we have been Democrat or Republican, Liberal or Conservative, the choice has always been the same and we have always made the wrong choice... larger government, which has more and more control over our lives, and higher and higher taxes, putting more money in the hands of government and less and less in the private economy.

Unfortunately, the decision we must make has now become even more complicated. After World War II, the most powerful and wealthiest people on our planet formed an organization, in secret at first, called the New World Order. The goal of this organization was to force the entire world to come together to be ruled by the United Nations. The New World Order is no longer secret. It is extremely extensive. You can buy a book at Barnes and Noble now which identifies many heads of nations as members and it also includes George Bush Sr., George Bush Jr., the Clintons, Obamas, Joe Biden, the heads of most large American corporations and most billionaires on planet Earth as well as many heads of government departments in the United States and members of Congress. It is my opinion that the only recent presidents of the United States who opposed the US becoming part of the world united under the control of the United Nations were Ronald Reagan and Donald Trump. We may still call ourselves Democrat, Republican, Liberal or Conservative, but the decision we make now is much more important than it has ever been. Not only are our leaders today asking us to turn over control of our entire lives to them, but they in turn are prepared to turn over control of our nation to world leaders. Unfortunately, these same world leaders are convinced that the way of life that we have enjoyed in America and other nations for our lifetimes is unfair to the rest of the world and should be taken away from us. If they are successful, democracy and capitalism will disappear from the planet. The society which they intend for us may not be called communism, it may be called Totalitarianism or by some other name, but it will be a communist system in which the government and the wealthy own and control all land, capital and means of production, and everyone else will live in poverty. It has become very difficult to know and understand how to vote in order to avoid unwillingly giving up control of our lives to these very wealthy and powerful people.

Will the New World Order ultimately succeed? They are actually very close already, as they are in control of many governments, certainly including the United States. They already have a plan to gain control of all money supply by diluting all currencies and creating a digital currency which they will have complete control over. They control the media and are creating incredible hatred for democracy and capitalism as being an unfair system that benefits only the wealthy. They have and are still using worldwide military power and opinion to displace government leaders who oppose the control of the United Nations and the New World Order. They are much closer to success than people believe or understand.

It is my belief that the New World Order will fail. I do not believe that it will ever be possible to achieve a consensus about who will be in charge behind the scenes. Why would individual government leaders be willing to give up the wealth and comfort of themselves and their own people to make everyone else wealthier and more comfortable? To a large extent, this has already been done in the United States and Western Europe. Trillions and trillions of dollars of wealth has been transferred from the middle class of these wealthier nations to Asia, India and Latin America through trade agreements that favor those nations. But it is not possible to make the world comfortable by stealing wealth from some nations and transferring it to others. Success in creating additional wealth for all lies in embracing the systems responsible for worldwide success and allowing it to spread worldwide. There are too many differences that exist among us that cause friction and over which we continue to kill each other. Religious differences remain a major source of conflict and will for a long time to come. Territorial control has been the primary reason for conflict and war. World leaders will not allow the United Nations to make these decisions for us. We have differences over how we live in society. People will not so willingly give up their right to own property and capital and decide for themselves how they live. These new trade practices that transfer wealth will cause conflict and war. Communism and democracy remain diametrically opposed. It is my belief that the New World Order will only create new reasons for conflict and war by forcing a way of life on people that they ultimately will not accept when they become aware of what is happening. Perhaps World War III is really being created for us.

Love,
Lawrence A. Stellato

Love Letter #12:
Crypto Whatever

April 14, 2022

Dear America,

A craze for investments in cryptocurrencies and the metaverse is sweeping the nation. It appears to indicate a great lack of understanding on the part of many Americans with regard to the inherent value of particular types of investments. Perhaps this letter may help many Americans understand where their money is going.

Substantial changes are taking place in the investment landscape worldwide. Purchases of cryptocurrencies, which seemingly began on a small scale by mostly retail investors, appear to be becoming more acceptable, in fact, to larger, more influential investors and even some funds controlled by large investment firms. It is easy to understand how the initial substantial increase in value of certain types of cryptocurrencies would entice new investors as a way to get rich quick. Early acceptance has also inspired some fund managers to create trading vehicles to allow these new currencies to be bought and sold more easily.

In addition to cryptocurrencies, very smart game creators see game players as a new source of revenue. They are creating a metaverse in which game players can buy uniforms, clothing, tools, weapons, land, and other things in an imaginary universe using, of course, real money. The purchasers of these imaginary properties and things are also hoping that others will come along later to pay even higher prices for the things they own in the metaverse. Both cryptocurrencies and the metaverse are offered as totally new and improved ideas for investment in the future. Many believe that these will be the most accepted investments in the future and will replace many of today's old fashioned investment vehicles. We need to look at the impact of these new ideas.

Perhaps we should take a new look at how we should see the intrinsic value of all the types of investments available to us in the new environment we face today and in the future.

• Maintaining cash is always an option. But increasing inflation is eroding the value of the U.S. dollar as well as many other currencies around the world, some much worse than others.

• Gold and silver have long been considered the best hedge against inflation and the value of these commodities have normally risen during times of inflation. This time, however, investors have begun to choose cryptocurrencies as an optional inflation hedge.

• Federal government bonds have long been considered the safest investment because lending money to the government carries the full faith and credit of the government to pay the loan. In recent years, interest paid on government bonds has been extremely low. It is my opinion that worldwide government debt has grown to the point that I do not believe any government on the planet has the capability to pay it back. In fact, it is my opinion that there is no government that ever intends to pay any of its debt back and, in fact, they all intend to continue to borrow more and more. To me, government debt has become the worst investment on planet Earth.

• Bonds of the states and bonds and preferred stocks of utilities offer higher rates of interest return than federal government bonds. Most utilities and some states are creditworthy and are still relatively safe investments. Some states are not.

• Corporate bonds represent the debt of corporations. Some have excellent balance sheets and their debt offers relative safety and a decent return.

• Investors buy and sell shares of stock of corporations on a large scale. New companies are constantly being formed and others are constantly failing, and the direction of worldwide economies keeps changing. The fortunes of corporations rise and fall accordingly, but the general direction of the stock market over long periods of time has been positive and wealth has been created for many. The stock market is still considered a good place to invest for long term gains.

Up to this point, we have looked at investments that have some apparent intrinsic value. Gold and silver have recognized value as commodities. Federal government bonds are backed by the government with a promise to pay. The U.S. dollar and other currencies have the support of their governments, and the U.S. dollar is still considered to be the safest currency for the determination of value of goods and services worldwide. Corporate bonds are corporate promises to pay. Many corporations could pay their entire debt tomorrow if they chose to. Shares of stock represent partial ownership of companies that own property and produce goods and services to create revenue.

Some very smart people have now created cryptocurrencies which, in my view, appear to have no apparent inherent value or backing. A crypto coin is an entry on someone's computer. We do not even know whose computer it is. It appears that anyone who can get people to trust him, can create a crypto coin, collect your real dollars and make an entry on his computer. He can charge you fees for this. In fact, other people are creating web sites on which transactions can be made and they charge fees also. It is difficult for me to accept that paying good money for an entry on some unidentified person's computer can turn out to be safe. In Canada, one of the largest traders of cryptocurrencies transferred hundreds of millions stored on his computer to his own accounts, faked his own death and thousands lost their entire savings, which are not guaranteed by anyone. It is true that, when we deposit our money in the bank, we are also turning our cash into a computer entry. But the bank is holding it for us.

There is government regulation and partial government guarantees. Some are coming to believe that government-backed cryptocurrencies will someday replace the currencies of all countries on our planet. That would improve the safety and reduce the volatility of them but, in my opinion, it is a very bad idea. I believe this will only happen if the currencies of all countries fail which, I also believe, will coincide with worldwide economic failure. Such worldwide economic catastrophe could result in 1000 years of Dark Ages, similar to the Dark Ages that came after the fall of the Holy Roman Empire. It is also my opinion that such total control over all money supply in the hands of the government which would be able to see every transaction would result in too much government control over our daily lives.

Very smart major corporations and individuals are also creating an imaginary metaverse. Many gamers already play in these imaginary game universes, in which we will now be allowed to actually buy clothing, tools, weapons, and property using, of course, actual cash money. They are doing this, of course, because they believe that some other gamer will eventually come along and pay a higher price in actual money for what they bought. We are once again being asked to pay actual currency for an entry on someone's computer. Presumably, the creator of the game gets to keep the purchase price. You cannot sell the property back to the computer and get your money back. I'm sorry, but I fail to see the actual value.

There is another very important point related to these investment issues that should be noted. These are all investment dollars. The entire worldwide economic system is based upon the system of capitalism which is subject to the laws of supply and demand. Demand for goods and services exists regardless of if there is any supply or not. The ability to produce necessary goods and services for the supply side of our economy relies upon the availability of capital. It appears that we are drifting further and further away from the idea of using our available capital to produce goods and services needed in our economy. Instead, we are using more and more capital to buy imaginary things in a metaverse or lend it to the government to give away to people which increases demand for goods and services we are no longer producing. In addition to this insane misappropriation of capital, we have also outsourced most of our supply to foreign countries which has apparently increased our shortages of needed goods due to their inability to supply the needs of U.S. citizens. Of course, we need to start bringing back production of goods to factories in the United States to insure availability for the needs of our citizens. But how should investment funds be invested in this country, not only for the safety of our investments, but also in the best interest of the U.S. economy?

• Gold and silver will continue to have value as commodities, although it may be questionable if they will remain the best inflation hedges in today's investment environment.

• Stop lending money to federal governments in such vast quantities. They are telling you that they will use it for roads and bridges, but they are in fact using it to devalue the currency and cause inflation that is destructive to the economy. We would be better off throwing it in the sewer.

• Some states are conservative, and utilities provide a valuable service and these can provide a decent rate of return.

• The government can devalue your cash on hand or in the bank but, until they turn it into a digital currency, they cannot take it away from you.

• Bonds of many corporations with good balance sheets can be relatively safe and provide a decent return on your investment. This investment money is also likely to be used to provide capital to produce the goods and services we need.

• Stocks of corporations are the major vehicle used in capitalism to provide capital to private companies for the purpose of producing goods and services. It is true that about eighty percent or more of all trades in the stock market every day are made by investment corporations, which control most of our investment funds, and they do not always use those funds wisely. This makes it difficult to choose the right investments. It is futile to try to guess what they will favor or sell at any given point in time. They all follow the same flawed rules. We must try to envision what the future direction of the country will be.

• Investments in cryptocurrencies and the metaverse appear to be idiotic. None of the money invested in these imaginary products is going to produce goods and services for our economy. If our economy fails because we are headed in the wrong directions, I am certain cryptocurrencies and the metaverse will vanish also.

In the United States in today's environment, my recommendation would be to try to find the correct apportionment of cash, conservative state, utility and corporate bonds and preferred stocks, and common stocks that fit best in your age and risk category. Gold and silver can also still be used as a traditional investment hedge. Federal government bonds, cryptocurrencies, and the metaverse do not fit in any portfolio.

Love,
Lawrence A. Stellato

Love Letter #13:
The Dangers of Nuclear Energy

April 23, 2022

Dear America,

Many years ago, at the start of my first career, I was employed by General Electric Company and graduated from the Financial Management Training Program there in Schenectady, New York. GE at the time was probably the largest manufacturer of power generators for the utility industry, and they had a huge backlog of orders for both fossil and nuclear power generators. The supervisor of the management program was so proud when he showed me what was the largest manufacturing plant in the world at the time, where parts for the generators were transported to be machined and prepared for assembly on site. It was an education for me about some of the elements of electric power generation. Today, very many electric utility generating plants exist, both fossil and nuclear, in probably every country on planet Earth.

It occurs to me that, as the world tries to eliminate all use of fossil fuels for power generation worldwide, a great deal of additional electric power will be required. Where will it come from? We are being told that we will be using renewable energy sources. It will be coming from the sun and wind. I'm sure some of it will, even though these sources of power appear to me to be more expensive than very readily available fossil fuels, which are still in abundance for the time being. But even just in the United States alone, I do not see how we can provide for the electrification of all our power usage, including transportation, using just solar and wind alone. Even if we cover every acre of farmland, forests and state parks with solar panels, will it provide the power needed reliably for all our homes, appliances, business needs, commercial transportation and the millions and millions of cars on the roads? Wind power will help but it is even less reliable than the sun. And, if we do this, where will our food come from?

Nuclear energy is also considered to be a cleaner provider of electric power than fossil fuels. It is my belief that the powers to be want much more of our power to be provided by nuclear power plants. We may have to build thousands of them around the world to satisfy electric power requirements. We have experience with nuclear power, as there are already many operating in many countries. But there have been failures. I remember serious meltdowns in Pennsylvania, Ukraine when it was part of the USSR and in Japan. These were serious nuclear accidents which threatened the lives of many people. Nuclear power is very dangerous. Since my working experience with General Electric, which is now long out of that business, I have often wondered how we came to be so receptive of nuclear power generation. When I worked in that business, I learned that nuclear generators create nuclear waste which gets stored in the Earth's crust and may take hundreds of years to neutralize. When last I read, nuclear waste in the United States is being transported to and is being stored in the Nevada desert. Will we be creating a huge amount of very dangerous radiation material and storing it in various places in the Earth's crust everywhere in the world?

I recently read that Germany and perhaps other countries in Europe were trying to phase out the use of nuclear power. In my mind, this is a very worthwhile goal. But they have been unable to replace it with solar and wind. Europe does not have its own supply of fossil fuels and must import what it needs. Here in the United States, however, we are lucky enough to have vast quantities of both oil and natural gas, which burns cleaner than oil or coal. Nevertheless, the current administration has severely limited the production of these fuels in an attempt to force a changeover to sun and wind too quickly. The result has been that the price of oil and natural gas has doubled over the past year or so and contributed substantially to rising inflation while putting many people out of very good paying jobs in those industries.

I am not saying that it is not worthwhile to change over to renewable energy sources to the extent that it makes sense to do so. Homes and businesses can be converted to more use of solar and wind in inexpensive and practical ways to some extent. Electric batteries that have the capability to store energy produced by sunlight are helping. Electric cars, however less useful and more expensive so far, are already on the road. But it is my opinion that it makes no sense to try to force this changeover to happen more quickly than possible at a cost of disrupting the lives of millions and millions and putting so many others out of work. If given a chance, our great economy will make this changeover happen automatically. As more practical forms of power become less expensive and others rise in cost, the changeover will occur. And we can spend our energy dollars in research efforts to improve alternative energy sources. We are blessed with a truly great economy that has the capability to improve the lives of so many worldwide in so many ways, but our administration always seems to choose to interfere. The result of that interference is always negative and extremely disruptive. And governments should not be imposing this increase in nuclear power on the planet.

Love,
Lawrence A. Stellato

Love Letter #14:
Interest Rates, Inflation, and Recession

May 1, 2022

Dear America,

Economics is a relatively complicated subject. Some definitions and explanations are required for those not familiar with the subject. The basic principles of economics are the laws of supply and demand. The price we pay for a product or service will rise or fall based on availability. Abundance of a product will generally hold down or reduce prices. Shortages will result in higher prices. Interest rates are the cost of capital. The last time we had very high interest rates was during the very bad inflation of the 1970s. The availability of capital has gradually increased continuously since that time which has resulted in gradually lower interest rates until this past year. It is important to note that interest rates affect both the supply and demand sides of the economy. Increasing consumer interest rates for credit cards, consumer loans or home mortgages will affect demand for products. Increasing interest rates for commercial mortgages, corporate bonds, and other commercial credit will reduce the capability of companies to provide availability of products and services for consumers and affects the supply side of the economy. Inflation results when demand exceeds the capability of companies to provide needed goods and services. Prices will rise as a result. Similarly, prices will stagnate or decline if an excess of goods and services exist. Gross Domestic Product is the total of all goods and services produced in our domestic economy. When Gross Domestic Product (GDP) declines for two quarters in a row, the country is deemed to be in recession. In fact, GDP did decline in the first quarter of 2022 for the first time in many years. If we have a similar decline in the second quarter, the United States will be in recession.

What is the present status of our economy, and how did it get that way? We have very substantial inflation or rapidly rising prices which means that demand for goods and services substantially exceeds available supply. How did it get that way? In the 1950s, when supply and demand were in balance in this country and every country on earth wanted to buy American-made products, everything we invented, used, ate, and shipped overseas was produced in this country. On the supply side, U.S. corporations have been sending manufacturing jobs from the United States to overseas countries since the 1970s. Jobs first went to Japan and other oriental countries primarily due to rising production costs at home. Later, during the Clinton Administration, trade agreements were reached to open free trade with China, India, Mexico and Canada. Many, many more jobs were transferred overseas from the United States as a result of these agreements. We have lost control over our supply chain as a result of these very substantial changes. I think everyone knows that nothing we wear or use is produced here anymore and very little of what we eat. Reliability of supplies from overseas has proven futile. Ports have not been expanded overseas or in the United States and supplies cannot get out or in. These shortages of supplies contribute to inflation.

It is also important to note that the United States government has borrowed almost $30 trillion since the year 2000. Most of that money is used for social programs, increase in government employment or other spending which increases the need for products and services to satisfy consumer demand. Such increases in demand which cannot be met by the supply chain are inflationary. Most economists, reporters and analysts today blame the increase in inflation on government spending. It should also be noted that, when Lyndon Johnson was President, he borrowed extensively from the Social Security Program to begin his social welfare programs showering vast sums of money upon the public which increased spending for goods and services which could not be provided by the supply chain that existed at the time. This was also largely responsible for the inflation of the 1970s. The inflation we are currently experiencing, as well as the inflation we had in the 1970s, are considered very serious problems that threaten future economic health and must be resolved.

Most economists agree, and college economics for the last three generations teaches that the solution to inflation is for the Federal Reserve Bank to increase interest rates as substantially as necessary to reduce the demand side of the economy and bring supply and demand back in balance which would correct the price inflation we are experiencing. I disagree. Raising consumer interest rates would dampen consumer demand, but raising interest rates in general also dampens supply and tends to cause recession.

The present conundrum, then, is how to reduce inflation without inflicting harm on our economy which, in my opinion, is already fragile. Don't forget that our government has injected almost $30 trillion into our economy of borrowed money which, if we had not done, might have resulted in lower Gross Domestic Products for the last twenty years. In other words, we may already have been in recession or depression for a long time. Raising interest rates alone may have no effect at all on inflation without affecting the economy in general. What we have to do is bring supply and demand back in balance by bringing production back to the United States thereby making our supply more reliable and available. Because of noticed shortages of chips, some chip manufacturers have committed to build new chip manufacturing plants in the Unites States. Car manufacturers are planning to build electric vehicles to be used in America here in this country while reducing the overseas production of gasoline vehicles. Changes of this type in the coming years will have a dramatic effect on reducing inflation. At the same time, such increased production at home will increase the level of employment in what has always been considered career jobs. This will have a very substantial effect on avoiding recession as well. It is important to note here that a substantial part of the increase in inflation we are currently experiencing has to do with a doubling of the price of oil and gasoline in the past year or so. These price increases, of course, are due to the current administration's efforts to curb the use of fossil fuels by prohibiting the production of petroleum and natural gas and shutting down pipelines. Petroleum is used in so many American products and gasoline and these increases added substantially to inflation. At the same time, we have eliminated many career-oriented jobs from our economy contributing to slow down at a time when we must defeat inflation without destroying our economy.

We must realize that the basic problem we have to solve

has nothing to do with damaging higher interest rates which would only tend to help further destroy the economy we are doing so much to slow down by sending jobs overseas for so many years and reducing production of petroleum in this country where we have abundance. Raising interest rates reduces both supply and demand. It has also been suggested that raising taxes could reduce demand. Nothing could be further from the truth. Increasing taxes dampens both supply and demand and contributes to recession. The problem we must solve is to increase supply to meet demand. We can make our supply of goods and services to meet consumer demand more reliable by bringing production back to this country. There is an immediate need to place restrictions on the importation of certain types of products from China and other countries, not only for purposes of improving our economy, but also for purposes of security. It is likely that much of our new technology as well as military capability is being given away by having everything produced by foreign countries, many of which are not even friendly or allied with U.S. interests. Lower taxes and lower interest rates are both beneficial to an expanding economy. Imbalance in supply and demand is not beneficially corrected by attempting to reduce demand. The correct solution to an inflation problem is to encourage our corporations to increase production here and bring jobs back to America. Interest rates need not be involved and should be affected only by the capital requirements of consumers and businesses. Recession will automatically be avoided if we go about correcting our inflation problem in the correct way and avoiding taking any action which will contribute to a recession.

Love,
Lawrence A. Stellato

Love Letter #15:
The Curse of Paul Voelker

May 12, 2022

Dear America,

America has always had a love affair with inflation. We love to see wages increase, home values rise, and stock market prices go up. Unfortunately, costs also rise, sometimes faster, and our wealth will actually decrease instead of increase. But we do want our inflation rate to be modest. When I studied economics in college, I felt that deflation was beneficial as it made American products more competitive worldwide. But this has always been a minority opinion. By definition, inflation exists when demand for goods and services exceeds supply which will cause prices to tend to rise.

During the 1970s, which most people are too young to remember today, we had a very substantial inflation. Most people considered it to be a wage inflation caused by strong unions. In my opinion, wage inflation does not just happen. It has a cause. People need higher wages because the prices of things they need to buy are going up rapidly and they have to house and feed their families. During that decade, Lyndon Johnson borrowed all of the money from social security to create his great welfare program. Giving all this money to people to spend created a great deal of additional demand for products and services. At the same time, taxes were increasing to support a growing war and an increasing federal budget. Increasing taxes on corporations as well as new prejudice rules about who to hire for the sake of equality and stronger unions combined to cause most United States corporations to move manufacturing operations to overseas countries. This substantially reduced the capability to produce products in this country to meet the new demand created by Johnson's giveaway program. It should not have been a surprise to anyone at the time that high inflation would result from these changes in government policy. But it became a major concern and was very substantially misunderstood.

At this time, Paul Voelker became Chairman of the Federal Reserve Bank, and in 1980, Ronald Reagan became President of the United States. Voelker announced something that had never been done before. He was going to cool off demand by increasing interest rates to rebalance supply and demand and thereby defeat inflation. He did raise interest rates to incredibly high levels. I can remember people getting mortgages at nearly fifteen percent interest rates and consumer credit became very expensive. But higher taxes on business and higher interest rates for commercial mortgages and bonds also penalized the corporations which supply our goods and would only increase their desire to offshore manufacturing. If you reduce both supply and demand, the result will not be reduced inflation, it will be recession and we did get a very substantial recession thanks to higher rates. Paul Voelker did reduce both supply and demand for goods and services and did cause a substantial recession but, in my opinion, he did not rebalance supply and demand as he promised and cure inflation.

So, what then did resolve the issue of high inflation and cause prices to stabilize? Reaganomics reduced taxes on the corporations that produce our products and encouraged corporations to remain on shore and produce goods here in this country. Doing so increased supply and made it more reliable, thereby helping to rebalance supply and demand. Interest rates have been gradually declining since until very recent times. It is my contention that it was Reagan's policies as President that solved the inflation problem and that Paul Voelker merely caused a deep recession, which may have contributed very little to the solution.

Unfortunately, during the Clinton administration, trade agreements were made which opened free trade with China and India and increased trade with Canada and Mexico. These agreements have once again begun a major offshoring of manufacturing that we need to be taking place at home to create lifelong skilled careers for American workers. And it has made supply unreliable. In addition, since the year 2000, the government has borrowed nearly $ 30 trillion and added it to our domestic economy substantially increasing demand for products that once again have come to be in short supply due to bad changes in government trade policy. So we once again have the threat of runaway inflation. It is interesting that each time this happens, it appears to be as a result of bad government policy. It is unfortunate that we seem to be dealing with the problem in the same way that Paul Voelker taught us. We will raise interest rates to oblivion if necessary to reduce demand, not realizing that we are also reducing limited supply even further which will definitely put us in recession. And everyone except the present administration seems to know that the added government spending is the primary cause of this inflation.

What, then, is the correct answer? We have to stop excessive government borrowing and spending. Reliable supply of additional products to meet the demand is not available. We must also focus on returning the production of goods needed in the United States to this country. Everything that we need in the

United States that can be produced here should be produced here. Importation is only necessary for products which cannot be made here but are needed. We have to focus on doing the things necessary to rebalance supply and demand in our economy. Interest rates are merely a cost of capital. They are not a tool to be used to control inflation or any other facet of our economy. This is the second time we have threatened to destroy the domestic economy of our country by changes in government policy and further destroy it by the tools we plan to use to fix the problem. Inflation is a very serious problem. The runaway inflation that we face again today is capable of total destruction of our economic system. How long will it take for Americans to realize that we have to insure that the changes we make in our government policy will benefit the local economy before we agree to make those changes. I hope this time that we can muffle the desire to raise interest rates and focus instead on real changes that will bring back the manufacture of goods to the United States and increase the supply available to meet demand. Creating good-paying manufacturing jobs here will also tend to expand the economy instead of working to create recession. The Federal Reserve cannot solve the problem of imbalance in our supply and demand. Unless we get very lucky by accident, there will be no "soft landing" that is hoped for by so many economists, forecasters, and analysts. Supply is very unlikely to increase to meet demand by accident. Reducing government borrowing and spending will reduce demand to a more normal level suggested by the economy, but we must also take steps to insure that we have reliable availability of the products needed for American consumers.

Love,
Lawrence A. Stellato

Love Letter #16:
Economics 901

May 18, 2022

Dear America,

From the time I studied economics in college many years ago, I have always believed that economics is as exact a science as math. Unfortunately, government has a habit of setting up a society, establishing economic principles, and then interfering with its proper operation. Wars are government interference in the domestic private economy. Substantial, unusual increases or decreases in defense spending are interference by the government in the domestic economy. Changes in trade policy between nations is interference by the government in domestic economic policy. A substantial increase or decrease in government employment compared to domestic employment is interference by government in domestic economic policy. If the government does not allow the domestic production of oil and natural gas and it has to be imported, there are domestic economic consequences. Welfare programs, though well intentioned, are a substantial interference in the economic management of the domestic economy. In my lifetime, I have not seen any evidence that our government, or likely any other government, takes into consideration the changes likely to occur when changes are made in government policy. Some guidelines need to be established.

The first and likely the most important guideline for the establishment of a sound economic system in any country is that the size of the government and its spending programs should not exceed the capability of the domestic economy to support it. If government at all levels and all of its programs exceeds twenty percent of the total gross national product of a country, it likely is borrowing to pay current and retired employees and its spending programs. Borrowing should only be required for infrastructure, and it is important to have a paydown program in existence for paying debt so that capital will later be available for additional infrastructure or rebuilding. There is probably not one country on planet Earth which has not exceeded this guideline. Excessive borrowing by government is damaging to the economy. It takes up and makes more expensive the capital required for private companies to produce the products and services required by the population. All excessive government spending, especially of borrowed funds, is inflationary and damaging to the domestic economy.

Military buildup and wars are a fact of life in today's world. It practically guarantees that no country will ever be able to provide the total capability for the best possible national welfare of its people that could result from its economy. Planet Earth never seems to run out of powerful people who feel that they have the right to tell everyone else how to live. Wars are fought throughout history to obtain control over other lands and people, over type of society in which to live, over religion, and over type of government and trade wars will soon result because of changes in government trade policies that have a dramatic effect on working class people in the countries affected. We are all aware of the economic damage and devastation that results from military buildup and war. No economic system could remain stable and provide the benefit it promises in such an environment. This is government interference in economics at its worst.

In recent centuries, trade practices have become a very substantial factor in economic policy. When the United States opened up free trade with China and India and increased trade with Canada and Mexico, it is likely that twenty or thirty million career manufacturing jobs were transferred to other countries from the United States. The United States has had trade deficits with other countries since the 1970s. Trade deficits are a transfer of wealth from the middle class of our country to other countries that have positive trade balances with us. We have been transferring jobs to other nations for very many years. This is substantial economic interference by the government in economic policy and affects the lives of the entire population.

It should not be a surprise that almost everyone believes that economics is not an exact science and that supply and demand cannot be expected to remain in balance according to economic principles. Government never seems to allow it. It is astounding to see how often a government, especially the United States government, will endorse and even enforce changes in economic policies that are extremely damaging to the economy of this country and its people. It certainly appears that the government of the United States, as well as many other governments around the world, are not really interested in the benefit of their own people. They appear to have other objectives. Many years ago, revolutions were fought and won to obtain the right for the people to elect leaders who would ensure that our nation is run for the benefit of the people. We have not done a good job. Politicians do a good job of hiding their true intent when they run for office, but we must strive harder to ensure that the leaders we elect have our best interests at heart. And we must learn to elect leaders who have knowledge of true conservative economics and will always put into practice policies that will benefit U.S. citizens.

Love,
Lawrence A. Stellato

Love Letter #17:
The Dangers of Cryptocurrencies

June 7, 2022

Dear America,

It is easy to understand how the increase in value of cryptocurrencies in the early days, which created an increase in wealth for many, has encouraged the incredible growth of interest in them that we are experiencing. Investment in today's day and age seems to embrace momentum trading in every investment vehicle. Nothing ever seems to trade at its real current value. Perhaps no one ever actually really understands or cares what that real value should be. I will submit an example from my own experience. When ROKU stock traded down to $70 a couple of years ago, I bought some shares, thinking that this company has a good future and the stock is substantially underpriced. When it got hot and was increasing in price, I sold shares at $160 and $200 thinking that it is now overpriced. The stock did not stop going up until it was at $470 a share. Today, it is around $90. This kind of momentum trading is accentuated by computerized algorithm trading that is taught in college master programs today. If you do not pay attention or care about what is happening inside your investment today, you can still make tons of money on the way up, but your portfolio will be devastated when it goes down. Even if you do study and understand your investments, the market will rarely price them at true current value. Unfortunately, about 90% of trades today are made by a relatively few investors who control the funds that contain the investments of most Americans. Prices of things will be what they think it should be whether correct or not. Today, they think that the market should be going down due to economic and geopolitical considerations, so that is where it is headed and almost everything is already underpriced. Dumbness pervades.

But the dumbest of all investors are those who believe in and encourage investment in cryptocurrencies. And they are becoming more and more accepted by major investors and even some bankers. Think about it. Buying a crypto coin is trading your actual real money for an entry on someone's computer. It is likely that you do not even know whose computer it is. No one guarantees the value of your computer entry or your coin or that it will be there if you decide to cash out. The manager of the largest crypto fund in Canada transferred a couple of hundred million dollars out of the fund into his own accounts, faked his own death and disappeared. A lot of investors lost their life savings. But the gigantic volatility and the inherent risk of crypto investments is not the primary reason we should not be making such investments. They represent a dramatic risk to the very democracy and capitalist system in which we live and which has provided the greatest society ever created on planet Earth.

Kathy Wood of Ark Investments recently was interviewed and was quoted as saying that we are experiencing in this country the greatest misappropriation of investment capital that has ever occurred here. I believe that she was referring to the fact that, in these bad economic times possibly upcoming, investors who control most of our capital run to hide in companies for reasons of safety that are not growth companies and sell investments in companies that likely have great futures and will grow well into the future. I say she is correct, but for a very different reason. Our great democracy and the capitalist system upon which our economy runs depends on the employment of capital for the production of the goods and services needed by consumers. We are talking about employing trillions of dollars of capital to invest in crypto coins which, not only have no intrinsic value, but also will not produce a single acre of tomatoes or a single washing machine to be used or eaten. This same theory applies to the trillions of dollars of capital which is planned to be used for creation of a metaverse. If we use all of our future capital to create computer entries of imaginary coins and images we see that are not real, where will future roads, bridges, tunnels, cars, groceries, appliances, buildings, homes and everything else we need to live come from? We have made and are making two major mistakes which have been and are going to continue to destroy the entire supply side of our economy. In addition to misemploying capital, we have exported the manufacture of everything we use in this country today to foreign manufacturers. Surely, it is obvious to everyone already that we have not been adequately able to rely on foreign countries to provide us with reliable supply of goods and services. When will we wake up and relearn to make everything we need right here at home. Imagine the inflation that this has already caused. Now we want to not use our available capital to produce goods and services here in the future to an even larger extent. Other countries will follow our example. Where will goods and services and modernization come from? Imagine the inflation, devastation of our economy and starvation that could be the result of these misappropriations of assets.

Cryptocurrencies also have other dangerous effects. Even if the government guaranteed the crypto and substituted crypto for currency, the danger would exist that the government would have too much control over our lives and how we use our money. In fact, it would provide the government the capability to raise taxes and take the money right out of our accounts without our knowledge or approval. No government should have that capability.

It is essential that Congress enact legislation to make cryptocurrency illegal as soon as possible and discourage the creation of the metaverse. All other countries should be encouraged to do the same. These are ideas that are potentially very damaging to capitalism and our democratic way of life.

Love,
Lawrence A. Stellato

Love Letter #18:
What Is Vladmir Putin Saying?

June 19, 2022

Dear America,

Vladimir Putin has been saying since before he invaded Ukraine that the United States is making it necessary for him to take such steps on behalf of the Russian people. In fact, since the end of World War II, Russia has been making statements that the United States has broken agreements made between the East and the West. After World War II, Russia gained control over half of Germany and many eastern European countries and formed the Union of Soviet Socialist Republics (USSR). Under that agreement, the Western European nations remained free of Socialist influence and became Democratic countries. But when the United Nations was formed, the United States, fearing communist expansionism, armed Western European nations and placed nuclear capability there. Russia was very upset, considered this a violation of existing agreements and, when Cuba became Communist, attempted to put nuclear weapons in Cuba which brought the world close to war. Over the decades since that time, Russia lost control over the eastern European bloc during the Reagan administration. In the meantime, the United Nations has made apparent huge numerous efforts to gain political and military control over many nations. If you join

NATO, you will come under control of the United Nations. If the United States, Canada and Mexico become united, the intention is that they will come under the control of the United Nations. If the World Health Organization gains control over worldwide health, will worldwide health then be under the control of the United Nations? Does the U.N., in fact, believe that planet Earth is overpopulated and intend to control the population by gaining control over world health? Vladimir Putin may believe that the United States has become the military arm of the United Nations and is setting a course to force all nations to come under the control of the United Nations including the United States. With the exceptions of Ronald Reagan and Donald Trump, all recent presidents of the United States have, in fact, been members of the New World Order and favor worldwide control by the United Nations. Vladimir Putin may be building his own empire to insure that his Russian Empire does not come under the control of the U.N. and the New World Order.

This is all speculation, of course. But it appears that we have to see the future of planet Earth in a new light. The world is being directed by many wealthy and powerful people in the direction of a New World Order in which the United Nations will rule the entire planet. It is no longer a question of simply a Cold War between communism and democracy—between socialism and capitalism. These differences in ideology still exist. And it does still appear that both Russia and Communist China intend to expand their communist empires to other nations and parts of the world. But we are all now also faced with the specter of control of the planet by the United Nations. It may well be that Vladimir Putin is expanding the Russian empire to resist having the United Nations being in control of all of Europe and at his doorstep. One of his demands of the Ukraine is that they should not join NATO and come under the control of the United Nations. I believe he sees the United States as the leading enforcement arm of the New World Order to bring control of the United Nations over the planet. The United States is, in fact, leading the arming of the Ukraine against Russian aggression.

Is the New World Order a good idea for mankind? It would appear that living on a peaceful Earth under one rule would be a good idea. What kind of world would that be? Well, we know that all ten of the leaders of the United Nations so far have been Radical Socialists and Communists or Totalitarians. In fact, they are the primary spreaders of the doctrine that capitalism is a very unfair system in which the wealthy take advantage of the poor and that the Western nations have victimized the poor nations of earth and stolen their resources. Nothing could be further from the truth. All changes in lifestyle that have improved the lives to some extent of everyone on the planet were invented in Europe and the United States because of the existence of capitalism and offered to all nations. The idea that the developed nations owe a transfer of wealth from their own countries to other undeveloped nations has no foundation in fact. The leaders of all nations have the same obligation to provide for their own people. If they do not do so, it is not the fault of the developed nations. It would seem that it is the intention of the New World Order to stifle the very creativity that has made the world a better place by eliminating democracy and capitalism. Rule by the United Nations may not be called communism. It may be called Totalitarianism or some other creative name, but it will be communism nevertheless. If all the land, capital, property and our health are in the hands of the government and the wealthy as is intended, then we are all slaves regardless of what the system is called. Very few people in the Western world would choose communism or totalitarianism over democracy if given a choice. Vladimir Putin may be doing us a favor by pointing out to us that we must also resist the expansion of control by the United Nations not only in Europe, but also worldwide. And he may be warning us that the United States is on the verge of handing control of our own country to the U.N. as well as helping the U.N. gain control over the planet. Many of our own leaders are believers in the New World Order... not only most recent presidents, but also the leaders of most of the agencies of our government. With the exception of Ronald Reagan and Donald Trump, all of the presidents of the United States in my lifetime have been believers in a united, one-world government under the control of the United Nations. And they have placed people in charge of many U.S. government agencies who have the same goals.

Will the New World Order succeed? I believe it will not. Too many world leaders will resist handing over control of their empires to the United Nations as Vladimir Putin seems to be doing. I do not believe that Communist China will ever bow to the UN and the New World Order. Other parts of the world will also resist. I am also convinced that, if the New World Order is successful, democracy and capitalism will be eradicated. So many people and their leaders cn this planet have embraced capitalism and it is not likely that they will permanently accept a communist or totalitarian way of life.

Love,
Lawrence A. Stellato

Love Letter #19:
Slavery

July 2, 2022

Dear America,

Slavery may be one of the most misused and most misunderstood words in the English language. Everyone in this country knows what slavery is said to be. Slavery is what we did to black African people when we brought them to the United States to pick cotton due to a need for labor in American commerce. No reference is ever made to who sold them to the United States. If they knew what the future would be for their progeny, they likely would have come voluntarily. Many Americans, ignorant of American and world history, likely believe this was a recent American phenomenon. Nothing could be further from the truth.

Everyone knows that there was no intelligent life on planet Earth in its very early days. Intelligent life here had very humble beginnings. Surely, early clans were led by alpha males who dominated and provided for the members of the clan. Were clan members slaves whose lives were controlled by their leaders? Clans spread out and became territorial kingdoms. Owners of the plantations supported the king who controlled the territory militarily. Were the serfs who worked the plantations for the owners not slaves? It is likely that slavery was essentially a way of life on this planet for eons until recent times. Territories became nations controlled militarily by kings. Was everyone who owned no property, wealth or capital not a slave?

Religious as well as world history contains many stories of slavery. Were the Jews not slaves of the Romans? The Bible tells us that Moses led them out of slavery to create a new nation of Israel. Oriental history is full of stories of leaders whose populations were effectively enslaved. World history has other stories of nations which have gained control of other nation's governments and the populations of the controlled nations are therefore effectively enslaved to some extent. Tyrants still exist today who rule their nations as kings and the populations of these countries are effectively enslaved.

In recent times, through revolution, people have claimed the right to elect their leaders. It was in this way that both communism and democracy were born. This very right to elect our leaders indicates some level of ascent from effective slavery. We no longer report to kings and lords. But, are there not some additional considerations? Communism does not permit the ownership of capital, land or wealth by the common people except as is approved by the government. Democracy allows the accumulation of land, wealth, property and capital by the population. Are those who live in Communist countries therefore, by definition, more enslaved than others who have those rights. There are many Communist countries today and the leaders of those nations have very strong military control over their citizens. It is difficult to tell the difference, I believe, between communism and the entire worldwide history of kingdoms that have ruled sections of planet Earth since the dawn of mankind. Slavery, it seems, needs to be more clearly defined.

There are most certainly many different levels of slavery and slavery has most certainly existed on the planet since the origin of intelligent life here.

There is no justification for the slavery that existed in the United States for a period of time. But it is no different or more unjustified than the slavery of the Romans over the Jews or the enslavement of almost everyone on planet Earth that has existed to one extent or another everywhere on our planet since the dawn of time. Slavery was not invented by the United States. It has always just been here and, in fact, still exists in various forms today. Families still sell their daughters into prostitution today. Is it not also true that there exists a New World Order today whose intention it is to bring all nations militarily and economically under the control of the United Nations? If the leaders of this movement are successful in bringing all of the nations of the planet under one control, would this not be some level of slavery? It will not be called slavery. It will not even be called communism. It likely will be called totalitarianism or by some other sophisticated name. But, if the rights of the people to own property, wealth, capital or control their own lives is taken away, then it is, by some definition, slavery. Here in the United States, our forefathers fought and shed their blood to earn these rights for us. Very powerful and wealthy forces worldwide today are conspiring to take them away. Control over property and other people has always been one of the most important reasons for conflict and war worldwide. It seems that the world will never be short of people who believe they have the right to control the lives of and tell other people how to live. We may always have to fight to protect the freedoms that were given to us, but it will always be worth the effort.

It is not unlikely that the people who were sold by their leaders to United States landowners as slaves to pick cotton may

107

have had a better life in slavery here than they had in early Africa. But most certainly, the acceptance of citizenship for former slaves and the economic gains they have achieved here since has been a great gift for all black people worldwide. Has American democracy and capitalism not saved the entire world from economic slavery? We must never let it slip away.

Love,
Lawrence A. Stellato

Love Letter #20:
Who Is Responsible for High Gas Prices?

July 9, 2022

Dear America,

So many different reasons are offered for the high gas prices we are experiencing. There is Russia's war against Ukraine. Some blame the oil companies for being greedy. We could say that OPEC is producing less to create shortages and keep prices high. Certainly, the fact that most of our world leaders want to transfer from fossil fuels to environmentally friendly fuels has something to do with it. We would have to be very blind to not see that very high gas prices and potential shortages of gas only occur during Democratic administrations. It was during the Lyndon Johnson and Jimmy Carter eras that we had the first dramatic price increases and shortages at the pump. Then came the huge price raises during the Obama administration. Now we have the Biden's highest price of all. It would not seem likely that there would ever be any necessity for high gas prices in the United States at all. It is reported that we have oil reserves in this country that are adequate for our needs for the next one hundred years. And that does not take into consideration the fact that we are already in the early stages in the process of changing over from fossil fuels to other forms of energy. It is also reported that we have about a one hundred fifty-year supply of natural gas which has also been escalating in price. Can there ever be any justification for any president of the United States to not allow production, pipeline distribution or refining capacity adequate for the needs of the people of this country? Can there ever be any justification for any president to allow the shipment of oil or natural gas to any overseas nation if we need it here? How is it that we ever elected any president or other public official who would do such a thing? Think about the inflationary impact on the budget of every American citizen that this is causing. What about the people we are putting out of good-paying jobs who would be working providing oil, natural gas for heating and gasoline at the pump for us? How can we justify an American president going to Venezuela, Iran and the Middle East to get more oil production while restricting production here at home? The United States is certainly one of the greenest nations on the planet and this decision to go overseas does not appear to help his goal of making the planet more energy environmentally friendly. There is a very high economic impact on every American as a result of these decisions. All of the presidents involved were Democrats and Liberals, but it is my opinion that this is not only a Democratic or Liberal problem.

Generally speaking, it appears to me that the thinking of Lyndon Johnson, Carter, Obama and Biden are merely in line with the goals of the globalists in charge of the New World Order. They do not feel that they were elected president as servants of the American people and to provide for the needs of the American people. Rather, they are agents of the New World Order whose goal is to bring new direction to planet Earth and I believe they do this knowing that harm will come to the

American people in the process. With the exception of Ronald Reagan and Donald Trump, all recent presidents of the United States have been affiliated with the New World Order. Clinton and both Bush administrations may not have caused drastic reductions in oil production in the United States to below America's needs, but other events occurred to further goals of the New World Order during their administrations. Trade deals that were approved by Congress during the Clinton era sent millions of American jobs to foreign countries. Wars seemed to further New World Order goals in the Middle East during the Bush Sr. and Jr. and Obama administrations. It appears that the disappearance of democracy and capitalism is a critical goal of the New World Order and it is happening in Latin America, the Middle East and possibly in African nations, Canada and Australia.

It would not appear that high gas prices are a goal of the New World Order. It only seems that they need to promote this problem to accomplish their goal of converting world power needs to different types of fuel. Even if a changeover to non-fossil fuels is a positive goal, it does not have to be accomplished overnight at the expense of economic hardship to many people in the United States and probably other countries as well. There is no reason to not continue producing as much oil as is needed while this transition takes place. My friends, it is becoming critically important to learn to elect officials to preside over us who have our best interests at heart. Politicians do make it hard for us to make the right decisions at election time because they are incredible liars but, in our lifetimes, it is becoming rare that we manage to accomplish this goal. If we cannot find ways to elect people who will have the best interest of Americans as their goal, our freedom, democracy and capitalism will surely disappear from our lives. The higher prices we are paying for energy today are the direct result of policies instituted by the Democratic and Liberal leaders we elected to run our government.

Love,
Lawrence A. Stellato

Love Letter #21:
Family Values

July 13, 2022

Dear America,

What is the origin of family life? How and why did it come to be? We all know that men and women must come together to have children so that mankind will have a future on planet Earth. I expect that, from the earliest stages, staying together as a family became the means by which men and women protected and grew their children into responsible adulthood. There are other relationships. There is a relationship between a man and a woman. There are relationships between friends. Gay men and women have relationships. Nations and governments have agreements and relationships for a common purpose. But these are not families. Family relationships developed over eons, it seems, for a particular purpose, which is, for the propagation of humanity.

All elements of society require rules, ethics, morals or values in order for mankind to live in harmony. All of the things being discussed here are very basic and you would think everyone is already aware of how society should operate. But it seems that all the definitions have changed. Perhaps we no longer understand what is expected of us. All of our original rules, ethics and morality came from the growth of religions. It seems that, from the dawn of time, mankind has believed that a God or Gods created the earth and all of us and has developed for us the rules by which we should live in society and this has become an important part of our culture. As families have always been the way we live in society, family values are a very important part of our culture. It would seem, then, that responsibility for raising children into responsible adults is the most important family value. As parents have become more and more absorbed in their own self-interest in modern times, it definitely appears that the primary responsibility of the family has become lost. In fact, the definition of what makes up a family is changing to include other relationships which are not basically families and do not have family relationship responsibilities by necessity.

Governments may be, at least in part, responsible for the confusion created around family life and family values. Many government officials seem to want to eradicate as much as possible religious beliefs. It seems that they would have us believe that only government has the right to tell us how to live and that we should not look to religion for our customs and culture. Of course, this would give government much greater control over our lives.

What religions teach us and government laws about how we should live in society are not always the same. It is very important that we have separation of church and state. History has taught us that, when religion has come to be too much in control of the government, persecution can result. But it is nevertheless important that religion should play a very important role in our society and our family life. The traditional family that consists of a husband, wife and their own children living together as a family at least until the children are grown into adults has practically disappeared in America. What has our society reaped as a result?

We have become the most crime infested country on planet Earth. Drug use has become an integral part of American life. Who can deny that tons and tons of illegal drugs come into this country and get used every year? We are accepting greater drug use as legal. Many states do not believe in prosecuting criminals. Some would rather prosecute citizens who try to protect themselves from criminals. Even if families want to stay together and teach their children to be responsible adults, to not become criminals or get involved with drugs, or to be responsible for their own families, how can we convince the children. Our own government is changing the definition of family. Our own government seems to be telling our children that proliferation of drug use is okay because people want it. Our own government is releasing criminals from jails and not prosecuting crimes. American society is breaking down. I blame the breakdown of family life and family values. Part of the cause is the apparent disappearance of religion in American life. Perhaps, religions should not rule our governments, but religious beliefs need to be part of what we teach our children as part of growing them to be responsible adults. The loss of family life and family values is a very great loss to American society. As a society, we need to bring the teaching of ethics and morality and the value of family life back into basic education in this country.

Love,
Lawrence A. Stellato

Love Letter #22:
Will Democracy and Capitalism Survive?

July 22, 2022

Dear America,

Friction and war seem to stubbornly persist on planet Earth. There are a number of reasons for war, some of which appear to date back to the origin of mankind. Men have been killing each other over religion for all of recorded history. Today, it appears to me that Islam is the primary religion being spread militarily in the middle east and by infiltration in other areas of the world. Control over people and domain—land and water rights—has been the reason, in my opinion, for most of the wars we read about in history. The two world wars appear to be the most extensive battles that have been fought for control over other nations and their people. In more recent history, rebellions resulted in the formation of democracies and communism. Communists espouse socialism and democracies prefer to allow property and capital ownership to citizens in a system called capitalism.

All recent wars seem to have been fought over the spread of communism and democracy. Even more recently, it is my opinion that the formation of the New World Order since 1947 by most of the richest and most powerful people on planet Earth has been the cause of all of the most recent wars and friction. The plan of the New World Order is to bring all of the nations on earth under the control of the United Nations. War is brought to depose national leaders who resist control by the U.N. We need to ask ourselves whether Vladimir Putin and Russia are fighting a war to bring Ukraine back under Russian control to improve his chances of maintaining Russia's ability to remain independent and resist control by the New World Order.

Since World War II, substantial changes in control over large sections of the world have taken place. After the war, Russia formed the USSR which included most of eastern Europe which became communist. China was also a Communist nation. This likely included almost half the world's population and attempts were made by both nations to spread their communist influence to other parts of the world and those attempts continue today. During the Reagan administration, Russia lost control over eastern European nations and progress was made in battling communist influence in Latin America. To complicate matters further, new trade agreements between the United States and China and other countries has brought partial capitalism to China. In addition, socialist ideals have spread to many democratic nations to the point where it is questionable whether capitalism truly exists in many democratic nations today.

Will democracy and capitalism survive? This has become a very complicated question. A lot will depend on the leaders of the New World Order and what direction they intend for the future of the planet. We must remember that all ten leaders of the United Nations until the present time have been radical socialists or communists. Certainly, they see Totalitarian control over the entire population of Earth as a worthwhile goal. The original leading promoter of democracy and capitalism worldwide until recently

117

has been the United States. However, with the exception of Ronald Reagan and Donald Trump, all recent presidents of the United States have been members of the New World Order. This does include George Bush Sr. and Jr., Bill Clinton, Barack Obama and Joe Biden. In my opinion, an examination of their presidencies will show dramatic tendency to subordinate the United States to U.N. rule and help the New World Order to subjugate other nations as well. It is interesting that these world leaders favored the trade changes made during the Clinton administration. Opening free trade with China and India and increasing trade with Canada and Mexico transferred many millions of jobs to other countries from the United States as well as sending trillions of dollars of wealth from the middle class of the United States to the middle classes of other nations. But it has also made China partially capitalist. This new capitalism brought tremendous new wealth to the Chinese middle class, but China is still fully controlled by the Communist Party which can take possession of all private capital there if it should decide to do so. That has already happened in all other Communist countries. Under the circumstances, if the New World Order is successful, capitalism will only survive if world leaders want it. It is likely that capital ownership would be reserved only for the very wealthy world leaders who support the new government.

Mankind has been on planet Earth for thousands of years, but democracy and capitalism are very new. In prior ages, progress in improving our lives has been extremely slow. A great deal of criticism exists about the inequality of capitalism, but it is my opinion that allowing ownership of property and capital in the hands of the common people is responsible for all of the great inventions we have seen in the past two centuries, which has potentially improved the lives of every person on our planet. It is possible that the deliberate disintegration of this system would send the world into a thousand years of dark ages similar to the era that existed after the fall of the Roman Empire. I also envision that communism and other forms of totalitarianism, in reality, are substantially more unfair than capitalism. If we agree to put all wealth, land and capital in the hands of the government and the wealthy few, surely we condemn ourselves to a life of slavery. Democracy and capitalism are essential to a decent life for the future population of our planet.

Will the New World Order succeed in gaining military control over the planet? I believe it will not in our lifetimes. Friction and war will likely continue to dominate our history due to differences in religion, social structure and government structure, and control over land of other nations. In addition, when it becomes widespread knowledge about how dramatically economic conditions are being manipulated by governments using new trade agreements, populations will likely rebel against their own governments which seem to be willingly causing new poverty at home to create better living conditions in other countries. Actions taken by world leaders to achieve their own goals often also is tending to change the balance of power between nations. Increasing the wealth of aggressive nations like China, which has expansion goals of its own, also has a tendency to promote more friction and war. Will the United States, as the military arm of the New World Order, promote wars to help bring more nations under the control of the United Nations? It occurs to me that world leaders do not understand how strongly people feel about and cling to the culture they believe in and the way they want to live. The best we can hope for at present is that people of different religions should live in areas where their religion is dominant. People who prefer communism should live in areas where that culture exists and make alliances with others who agree with them. Others who prefer democracy and capitalism can live where it is accepted and form alliances with other nations that agree. Eventually, long after we are all gone, perhaps all of the people of planet Earth will come to agree on a common culture and be able to live in peace and harmony. At the present time, it does not seem possible, but it seems that we never run out of egomaniacs who feel they have the right to tell everyone on our planet how to live. The world is not ready for their brand of globalism which, at the present time, would surely be global totalitarianism.

Love,
Lawrence A. Stellato

Love Letter #23:
Thank You, Bill Clinton

August 2, 2022

Dear America,

Let me at first say that everything I write is based on my own observations and represents my own opinion of the state of United States affairs. I offer no evidence to substantiate my opinions. This letter is basically about the transportation industry which appears to owe a great debt of gratitude to Bill Clinton.

During the Clinton administration, congressional approval was obtained for new agreements which opened up trade with China and India and substantially increased trade between the United States and Canada and Mexico. The result of these new agreements, whether intended or not, transferred millions of jobs from the United States to these other countries. You would be hard pressed today to find anything you need, use, drive, live in or even eat today which is totally made or grown in this country. At the same time, however, no apparent preparations were made to improve the ports, railroads or transportation systems in the country that would be needed to bring all these goods into our nation and transport them to where they are needed. This has to be a huge boon for worldwide transportation. Thank you, Bill Clinton. Transportation costs have increased geometrically, of course, as a result.

Unfortunately, this is not the only detrimental effect on the U.S. economy. Millions of manufacturing jobs that support American families were also transferred to other countries. It does also appear that a lack of supply has contributed substantially to the increase in inflation we are all suffering through today. More pain is coming as the Federal Reserve increases interest rates to fight the inflation in our current economy.

My friends, it just appears to me that we are electing public officials that do not have the best interest of the U.S. general public at heart. It seems to me that the current pain being experienced more by the poor in this country than anyone else is caused by our own recent government administration. We are being lied to as we are being told that these actions are in our best interest. We need to learn to read between the lines when these top public officials make promises to us. We need to learn to better anticipate the detrimental effects that will result from these changes in public policy.

Love,
Lawrence A. Stellato

Love Letter #24:
Unemployment Rate

August 8, 2022

Dear America,

It has been my belief that the United States economy has been in recession since about the 1990s. I understand it is not commonly understood to be the case, but it is my opinion. Our government has borrowed about $30 trillion since that time and given it away to people to spend which has inflated our GDP numbers. I do not believe that this spending in any way created new manufacturing jobs here or grew our economy. Everybody knows that we have been sending jobs from the United States to other countries since the 1970s and, after a brief hiatus during the Reagan administration, began to send many more overseas again after the trade deals of the Clinton administration. Under the circumstances, how can I draw any conclusion except to believe that the U.S. economy has been in recession for many years? We need to examine whether we truly have 3.6% unemployment here in this country.

I was raised during the late 1940s and 1950s, and I will draw some comparisons between the economy of that time as I remember it and the economy of today. In the early fifties, my memory is that the population of the country was about 180 million, and about 120 million were employed, or about two-thirds. Today, the population is over 330 million, and about 140 million are employed, or about 42%. In our domestic economy in the 1950s, almost everything we used, drove or ate was produced in this country and we were exporting to every country on the planet because everyone wanted U.S. products at the time. Today, everyone knows we import almost everything we use and much of what we eat. In the 1950s and 1960s, all our cars were made in the US. Today, all the parts come from overseas. Inflation may have made our numbers larger, but our economy is smaller. It does not appear possible that, with only 140 million people employed, that we could have such a low unemployment rate. One hundred forty million workers could not support our very fat nationwide governments and all their retirees plus one hundred ninety million non-working Americans. That is a large part of the reason, it seems, that we have such very large deficit spending and borrowing. About 220 million Americans would have to be employed to have comparable employment to what existed many years ago.

We know that living standards are better today for many people than what existed in the 1950s. Many more people are retired, a lot of them comfortably. But surely, there are 30-40 million Americans that would be working and planning for their future retirements if we had maintained jobs for them here in this country instead of shipping so many of our best family-supporting jobs to overseas countries. Surely, there are 30-40 million Americans who are of working age and ability who are not working and not being counted as unemployed. It is my understanding that we even hire from other countries many of our best paid employees in our great technology companies instead of American citizens. This is likely due to prejudice laws created in the 1960s and 1970s which prevented Americans from being allowed to study the special skills required for these jobs in colleges and universities. If we add the 30-40 million to our unemployed who should be counted, our unemployment rate would be somewhere between 22% and 27%. Who are these 30-40 million people who could be working but are not? Are any of them making any money? Nobody seems to know, but I will speculate about who some of them might be.

Millions of them might be illegal migrants. Everyone knows there are millions of them in the country. Some are not working and being supported to a large extent by the government or others. Certainly, tax dollars pay for their health care and, in many cases, transportation, at least temporary housing and other welfare. Many are working but, because they have no legitimate social security cards, may not be counted as either working or unemployed.

There was a time when assistance for young people who wanted to get a college degree was very limited or totally unavailable. Young people went to work right after high school for the most part and a lot of higher education was achieved in night school. Today, we have much greater promise and free education for athletes. We have much more availability of tuition assistance. And students have borrowed over a trillion dollars for tuition payments which is still outstanding. Many are now realizing that the jobs which they were supposed to have available to them after graduation from college have been transferred to other countries and they are hoping the government will tax other people to forgive them their debt. I have a grandson who got his first full time job at twenty-four years old. I understand he just got a two-year degree from college at twenty-five years old. So many of our young people today do not go to work until mid or late twenties for a myriad of different reasons.

The structure of our workforce is changing. We need to bring back the jobs that create futures for our young people and enable them to support their families which they are hesitating to create and finding hard to support.

Tons of illegal drugs come into this country every year through several different ports of entry. People do not talk about it, of course, but in my opinion, this importation must be arranged by, supported and paid for by wealthy people in America. These drugs are transported to and sold in every city and state in this country. This is, of course, primarily done by unemployed people. There are, of course, also many addicts which are also likely unemployed. We all know that addicts who have children are also supported by the government. It is unlikely that many, if any of these people, are counted in employment numbers.

I draw two very important conclusions from the facts stated here. The first and most important fact is that we have to learn to hire much better managers to run our country for us. People whose only expertise seems to be to know how to export jobs to other countries do not belong in the management of this country. How can that possibly be in our best interest? People who only seem to know how to grow government to larger and larger sizes until it can no longer be supported by the economy of our country do not belong in our management. They are only helping themselves at the expense of workers and taxpayers. People who only know how to borrow money that they never intend to pay back and only seek to borrow more and more until we run out of borrowing power do not belong in charge of our government. They are bankrupting us. People who only know how to promise giveaway programs that cannot be paid for to get themselves elected do not belong in charge of government. They only care about themselves. People who do not understand basic economic principles do not belong in charge of government. They do not even consider the impact that their policies will have on the population and on our daily lives. Wealthy and powerful people who endorse the New World Order under the control of the United Nations should not be in charge of our nation. It is their goal to enslave the population of the world.

The second conclusion that I draw from the facts stated earlier is that we need to restructure the way our government reports economic results to us. The current administration is placing great emphasis on the fact that our economy is extremely healthy due to the fact that we have such a low unemployment rate. Nothing could be further from the truth. Substantial incorrect decisions could be made on the basis of this misinformation. The economy will be mismanaged, of course, but the greatest error of all will be that we might maintain our current management in government. I do not believe that there has ever been a time in the United States when we ever needed a more extensive overhaul of the management of our country. When we go to the polls today, we need to have learned who has the best interest of the American people at heart. They are the only ones who deserve our votes.

Love,
Lawrence A. Stellato

Love Letter #25:
United States Central Bank
Digital Currency

August 19, 2022

Dear America,

On March 9, 2022, President Joe Biden issued Executive Order 14067, apparently for the purpose of "Ensuring Responsible Development of Digital Assets." The investment in cryptocurrencies has been growing dramatically in recent years, and it is essential for the government to insure responsible development of such assets. I should emphasize that, in my opinion, no investments in cryptocurrencies are in the best interest of the United States economy. We have a capitalist economy in which we invest capital in companies or entities which produce goods and services required by consumers. Investments in cryptocurrencies produce no such necessary goods or services and are therefore misuse of essential capital in our economy. Nevertheless, if they are to exist, they must be responsibly managed.

However, Executive Order 14067 also includes a Section IV entitled "Policy and Actions Related to United States Central Bank Digital Currency." This section refers to something completely different. It calls for studying whether we should actually replace the United States dollar with a digital currency issued by the Federal Reserve Bank. Section IVb directs all government agencies to report back to the president on the impact that would result from this change. This means, of course, that President Biden is actually considering making this change. In fact, Section IVbvii instructs government agencies to include instruction on how this change could support monitoring or mitigating climate impacts and grid management.

The United States would not be the first country to make such a dramatic change. To the best of my knowledge, however, the only countries making such a change would be because their currencies have collapsed due to dramatic uncontrolled inflation. By now, surely everyone knows that inflation is primarily caused by government interference in the local economy. Runaway inflation and the collapse of the local currency normally accompanies the total collapse of the local economy. This is happening in certain countries in the world today. Substantial inflation is a danger in Western Europe, Great Britain and the United States today, where steps are being taken to bring it back under control.

When President Biden attempts to put this currency change in effect, which I have heard may be in the next few months, he will try to sell it to the American people as a positive step for the country and an effort to keep the United States in the forefront of technology worldwide. In my opinion, however, a central bank digital currency is the most ingenious device ever created on planet Earth to enable governments worldwide to control and enslave the population. Right now, you can have cash in your home, in a safe deposit box, or make purchases in cash privately or you have money in banks or investments that the government has very limited knowledge about. Converting all of your money to a digital currency will give the government full and complete knowledge of everything you have and every dollar you spend or earn. This is extremely dangerous. Right now, the government cannot take your cash away from you or take your money out of your account at the bank or from an investment account. A digital currency would make things very different. What would keep the government from knowing where you are at all times and what you are buying every day. If the government did not want you buying gasoline because it harms the environment and decides to tax you exorbitantly for such purchases, what would keep it from removing the money directly from your accounts. It is my opinion that the primary purpose for creating such power for government would be to use it to entirely eliminate the middle class and equalize living standards for all. They would be able to create a Totalitarian state in which they could dictate how we live and only government officials and the very wealthy who the government appoints to provide goods and services would be in control of all assets and means of production. Perhaps, eventually, all property as well.

We all want to believe that we live in the United States of America and that our elected officials would never take away our constitutional rights in this or any other way. Unfortunately, that is no longer true. Today, there is a New World Order intent on establishing a worldwide Great Reset with the intention that all nations and all people will be brought under the control of the United Nations seemingly whether they want it or not. The goals of the New World Order, it seems, are to reduce the population of the planet and to impose a new living standard and rules upon the general population which they feel are more in line with what they feel are planetary requirements. The United States is not only not exempt from these goals, but it has become a leader in establishing worldwide compliance. We have to consider that most of our recent presidents including Jimmy Carter, George Bush Sr., George Bush Jr., Bill Clinton, Barack Obama and Joe Biden are all leaders in the Great Reset and have devoted their administrations to these goals. Only Ronald Reagan, who once threatened to remove the United States from the United Nations and Donald Trump, who announced to the United Nations during his presidency that globalization is dead, favored the United States as remaining an independent nation not subject to the United Nations. It is my opinion that, if this step is successfully accomplished and all other nations follow in digitizing their currencies, the final goal of world domination and enslavement by the New World Order will have been accomplished and the freedom and independence enjoyed by the American people and many other nations around the world for so long which was fought for by our forefathers so many years ago will have been lost forever. All of the heads of the departments of our government that will report to the president and make recommendations are non-elected officials and are likely to recommend this change. It is essential that we make our leaders aware that we oppose this change. It is equally important that we become much more adept at electing officials to run our government that have the best interests of the American people at heart.

Love,
Lawrence A. Stellato

Love Letter #26:
Global Warming

August 22, 2022

Dear America,

If we are able to look up into the night sky, we would see perhaps millions of stars. Each of these stars is likely a solar system similar to the one in which we live. In my book, *Past, Present, and Future of Planet Earth*, I make reference to the fact that the universe is so large as to be not only beyond our knowledge but perhaps beyond our comprehension as well. While the importance of the earth is substantial to us because we live here, it is nevertheless not even the tiniest pebble in the universe.

Planet Earth has been in existence for eons. Intelligent life is only recently here. During its existence, religion, science, history and geography tell us that many enormous ecological events have taken place here. Religions tell us that there was a great flood. They tell us that the planet existed long before intelligent life arrived. A god or gods ruled our planet and made very substantial changes here. Dinosaurs who ruled the Earth were made to disappear. Historical records tell us that there was an ice age. There have always been hurricanes, fires, volcanic eruptions and other natural disasters, and there is no evidence to conclude that these events did not occur before mankind existed on this planet. There is evidence that great rivers existed where there are deserts now. Some continents may have been closer together and others further apart at one time. Many ships have disappeared in the Bermuda Triangle. Perhaps damaging storms always existed in that region, even before mankind. Meteors have occasionally hit Earth. There have been great dust storms including one in the United States in the early 20th century. History tells us that friction and war has caused great destruction on our planet. We can speculate that planets may not have always been the same distance from the sun. Do we know if the sun has always been the same temperature, and if it will always be? We certainly have to acknowledge that our planet has always undergone dramatic transition, before and after mankind and that mankind played no part in a great deal of it. That does not mean, of course, that global warming is not occurring now on Earth or that it is not caused by the way we live. It should tell us, however, that it is a very minor event by comparison to many of the other natural disasters the planet has faced. It also should make us aware that we could solve this problem and a meteor would hit us next week and split the planet in two. We are at the mercy of nature more than we would like to believe. Nevertheless, we have to do the best we can to make life on Earth as good for us as we can.

I have been alive for more than seven decades. When I was very young, I can remember people predicting that, by now, Florida and the west coast of California would be underwater because the icebergs were melting. They have been melting ever since, but the effect seems to have been overstated. Scientists disagree with each other and it appears that, at times, none of them are correct in their predictions. Nevertheless, the

Industrial Revolution has brought many changes to our planet. We have learned to use power to improve our lives. We created hydroelectric energy to provide light and heat. We changed the course of rivers and built dams to enable this altering where many people lived. Since that time, we have learned to use sun and wind to harness some additional electric power. Presumably, the powers to be have not considered the impact of these changes to be damaging to the environment. We have also discovered that nuclear energy can be used to provide electric power. Nuclear power is used in many countries around the world and, at present, is not considered a danger to mankind.

More recently, we have discovered that oil and natural gas, abundant in the earth, can provide power in a different way. Burning oil and gas can be used to operate engines which have many different applications. Burning oil and gas adds chemicals to the atmosphere that are considered dangerous to our environment. As a result, governments on earth are making changes which will cost many trillions of dollars resulting in dramatic economic consequences. These changes will also alter the way of life of every living human being.

Based on current knowledge, there are four basic sources of power presently in use to power our way of life... hydroelectric, nuclear, coal, oil and natural gas and sun and wind. There are nearly eight billion people on Earth today and, although the wealthy and powerful are trying to reduce the population because they are likely correct in their belief that the earth cannot provide a good life for so many, it is possible that the population may continue to grow. We need to examine the benefit and danger of each source of power to society.

We are probably already using all of the hydroelectric power that can be created from existing resources on our planet.

This is not generally considered to be a danger to the environment, although some displacement of people took place during construction of the dams and diverting rivers.

Nuclear power has been being used for decades and nuclear plants to generate electricity exist in many countries. Nuclear power, while it is considered to be a clean source of electrical energy, is extremely dangerous. There have been meltdowns in Pennsylvania in the US and in Ukraine and Japan. Nuclear energy production also creates nuclear waste, which is extremely radioactive, must be stored in the earth's core and can take hundreds of years to neutralize. Some countries would like to stop using nuclear energy, but sensibly speaking, if we eliminate the use of coal, oil and natural gas as is being planned, we likely will wind up with many more nuclear plants.

Sun and wind are the sources of choice for future creation of electric power to replace the use of fossil fuels. It would be foolhardy to even imagine that we can generate enough power from sun and wind to replace the fossil fuels we use today, or that they will provide power as reliably. Sun is not out on all of the Earth all day every day and wind is even less reliable. It is likely taking a great deal of fossil fuel energy to build all of the solar panels and wind turbines for future use. These sources do provide clean energy for the environment during operation. It is my belief that the powers to be that are guiding these changes are aware that these sources cannot replace fossil fuel use and expect us to be living very differently in the future as a result of the changes they are making. If only the wealthy drive and the rest of us are all expected to live the same way in much smaller dwellings requiring much less power, energy requirements will be greatly reduced. I believe that this is the lifestyle planned for our future.

It is estimated that the United States has proven reserves of oil to last for the next one hundred years. We have natural gas reserves for one hundred and fifty years. Coal is very abundant. These resources do pollute the environment to some extent, but it has been proven in the United States and other places that the pollution can be reduced and controlled. I can remember polluted air in Los Angeles, New York, and the Midwest that I experienced myself. I remember Love Canal and other rivers and lakes that were polluted, but have since been cleaned up. It is sad that the United States and Western Europe, which have dramatically improved environmental management, no longer manufacture products. All manufacturing and pollution-creating activities have gone to developing countries which are given a pass and allowed to continue to pollute. Many trillions of dollars are being spent to make these changes and many new jobs will have to be created to replace the jobs lost by eliminating fossil fuels. The resultant government borrowing and spending is causing major inflation issues worldwide, and the raising of interest rates by federal reserve banks worldwide to fight inflation is causing and will continue to cause worldwide economic recession.

If climate change was as dangerous as scientists and governments make it out to be, half of the population of Earth would already be dead. We are causing damage to air and water, but it has proven to be fixable and controllable. We certainly should do everything we can to produce goods to satisfy the needs of the population as safely as possible. Sun and wind should be used to the extent that it is practical. But, if we use up all available land to create solar panel fields to produce electricity, where will our food come from? This is very different than just putting solar panels on homes and businesses to help assist in energy needs. If allowed to do so, the economy, without any interference, would create necessary transition. The government could help with research to help make cleaner energy less expensive, and fossil fuels would phase out as they are not needed. Government intervention to force change never seems to fail to generate economic destruction. We need to develop a commonsense approach to this problem. Current world leaders seem to be in an incredible hurry to ban all fossil fuels from use long before we have the capability to replace their use with alternative energy sources. We can improve the production of energy on our planet and use it in better and safer ways. And it makes sense to do so as expeditiously as we can. Our economy will help us accomplish this goal in the long run. But all nations must be asked to contribute to this effort in a fair way, and we must make every effort to continue to provide for the needs of the population until alternative energy sources are available to meet our needs.

Love,
Lawrence A. Stellato

Love Letter #27:
Conflict and War

August 31, 2022

Dear America,

With the exception of 9/11, Americans have not faced actual conflict right here in our homeland since the Civil War. We have sent soldiers to fight all over the world, but it has not come home to threaten our lives and our homes. But world history is not a history of life on our planet. It is a history of conflict and war.

Everyone knows that the planet existed long before humanity arrived. Animals ate each other for lunch and dinner, but it was an otherwise peaceful place. When mankind arrived, however, and gradually took possession of Earth, things changed. There are a number of reasons why mankind is so volatile that we will discuss here, but the focus of this letter is to emphasize that mankind is irrationally warlike. It seems that we will never run out of people on our planet who believe that they have the right to control others and tell everyone how to live.

From the very beginning of civilization, conflict has taken place in which humans fought over the control of land…hunting grounds, water rights and crop areas. The law of the jungle surely was original law. The alpha male ruled and protected the group and made the rules. Throughout history as populations grew, all societies were created through war and conquest. In more recent times, World War I was an attempt by Germany to take control of all of Europe. In World War II, Germany again attempted to take control of large segments of the world while Japan attempted to take control over all oriental nations. Still today, all nations have their own military and military alliances to protect their borders from invasion. There is, in fact, today an even greater threat to the sovereignty of all nations on the planet in the form of the New World Order. This new threat began in 1947 after World War II as a secret organization with the goal of enlisting many wealthy and powerful people and their children for the purpose of eventually subjugating all nations of Earth under the control of the United Nations which was formed at that time. So, the first reason for conflict and war was to gain control over other people and their land, and this continues on an even larger scale to this day. It appears that there is no new land available to fight over. All of the planet is occupied. So now, we fight over who will control it all.

The earliest history of our planet comes to us through religious records which are also the earliest sources of ethics and morality. As intelligence in mankind began to grow, we began to assume that our planet and all of us were created by some almighty deity or God. We assume that our God had the right to rule us and tell us how to live and this belief began to replace the laws of nature and became the rules by which we live in society. But so many religious beliefs grew throughout history. And all religions had their own hierarchies. So many different societies resulted. Religion became the second major reason for conflict and war on planet Earth. Although Jews, Christians and Muslims all believe in and honor the same God, wars over religious belief fill history books. Islamic Middle

139

East nations hate Israel and have gone to war to eliminate it as a nation. Radical Islamists invade and conquer villages in many countries including Africa, India, the Middle East and southern Europe and spread the Muslim religion through war. Christian and Muslim wars are legendary. Jews integrate into other societies and bring Judaism with them. Catholics, Protestants and Greek Orthodox Catholics all disagree over religious tenets and persecutions and wars have resulted. Buddhist and Hindu religions also created rules for societies in oriental countries and India. Greek and Roman gods lived in the skies and were also warlike. Religious beliefs are deeply imbedded and resistant to change. Religions have been a major source of friction and war for many centuries

Originally, all societies on planet Earth could be described as kingdoms. From the earliest groups ruled by alpha males until recent times, mankind lived in kingdoms. A king ruled militarily, the lords owned all the land and means of production and supported the king, and everyone else was a serf and worked for the lords. Several centuries ago, revolutions took place in Western Europe and Russia where the people ousted kings and new societies emerged. The idea was spreading that the people created products and should share more substantially in the profits created. Democracy and communism were born. Democracy spread to many areas of the planet because European nations had colonized many areas of the world. But both Russia and China, which had both embraced communism, attempted to spread communist influence into Eastern Europe and other oriental countries. Wars were fought by Western nations to attempt to halt the spread of communism. So, the third major cause of war on planet Earth has been type of government under which people want to live. Russia has also attempted at times to spread communism into the Middle East and Latin America.

Communist societies are socialist. While they have the right to elect members of their government, members of socialist societies have no right to own property or the means of production and only those approved by the government to produce products and services are permitted to accumulate wealth. Democracies embrace a capitalist system in which any person may own property, produce goods or services and accumulate wealth. Socialism and capitalism are very different types of societies and major conflicts have arisen over these ideological differences. Many wealthy and powerful people contend that capitalism leaves too many people behind economically and is unfair. If this powerful group is effective and subjugates all nations under the control of the United Nations, it is likely that capitalism will be dramatically muted. Many others understand that it is likely that all progress that humanity has seen in recent centuries has arisen because of the capitalist system. Capitalism is responsible for the birth of all inventions in the industrial revolution because average people are rewarded for their benefits created for mankind. Would we still be basically a worldwide agrarian society if capitalism never existed. Nevertheless, economic differences between socialism and capitalism remain a major impetus for conflict at present and for the future.

Major improvements in transportation have dramatically increased trade between nations. As economic conditions in Western nations substantially increased wealth and cost of production in those nations, trade agreements were made which allowed corporations in wealthier nations to produce goods for their home countries in countries where those goods could be produced less expensively. This has created large trade deficits in many nations which have persisted in some cases for fifty years or longer. A trade deficit is the transfer of wealth from the middle class of the deficit country to countries which have positive trade balances with it. The United States has been a victim of such trade deficits since about the 1970s. The transfer of middle-class wealth takes place because you are creating jobs to produce your goods in other countries instead of at home and you are becoming a purchaser nation instead of a producer. These changes, which have been taking place for the last few decades, are transferring economic power from Western democratic nations to Communist countries which are getting bolder and more powerful militarily as a result. This is another major impetus for conflict and war.

Despite the tremendous economic and technological growth that has taken place on our planet, it does not appear that there is any reduction in the probability of conflict and war. Militaristic spread of Islam is growing. Communist nations, despite relatively recent setbacks in the 1980s, continue to spread communist influence into other nations and areas of the world and have become more economically and militarily powerful and able to do so. The New World Order has invested heavily to influence control of governments worldwide by believers in the benefits of world control by the United Nations. With the exception of Ronald Reagan and Donald Trump, all recent presidents of the United States have seemingly devoted their administrations to assisting in this effort by adding new members to the United Nations, NATO, PANAM trade agreements and others. All departments of the U.S. government appear to be on board in this effort. The U.S. military appears to be ready for use in efforts against any nation who opposes this totalitarian effort. Major leaders around the world will continue to resist this effort, and it certainly will contribute to the likelihood of additional conflict and war.

What can be done on planet Earth to reduce friction and chaos and lead to less conflict and war? The primary goal, of course, has to be to eliminate the desire of the rich and powerful who feel that they have the right to tell everyone on Earth how and where to live. They actually are the cause of friction. Let's look at the causes of war individually:

Conquest... the most common cause of war has been the conquest of other lands and people. Predator nations like China and Russia will continue to prey on weaker countries. Target countries need to build military and economic alliances with stronger nations that have common interests. Unfortunately, it is still only military strength that will deter predator nations. We all pray the day will come when all nations respect the right of others to choose their own way of life.

Religion... religious beliefs run deep. You should live where your religion is accepted and common. If you choose to go to another country where it is not common, do not take your religion with you. Nations with a common religion have a natural bond and alliances will likely work well.

Government... Communist governments have been and remain overly aggressive in their attempts to gain control over other nations. We should not be trading with Communist nations or transferring economic power to these countries. Each nation has the right to choose the type of government that will rule it's people. The wealthy and powerful attempting to help the U.N. gain full control over the planet must be convinced to understand that they cannot impose their will on everyone. Many leaders will continue to oppose their efforts. We must especially elect officials here in the United States who have the best interests of the people of the United States at heart and who oppose world conquest.

Economics-world opinion at present and for the last few decades appears to be that democracy and capitalism provide too much control to the people and that governments must retake control over the population. The wealthy and powerful have control of the media who appear to support this effort by changing history. It must become better known worldwide that all of the improvements in our lives have come to be as a result of democracy and capitalism. The industrial revolution did not take place in Russia or China. It did not take place in India, Latin America or Africa. The industrial revolution that resulted in all inventions that have improved the lives of the citizens of the entire world to some extent or other happened in Western Europe and America where democracy and capitalism made it possible. Rather than eliminating capitalism and democracy from the planet, we must allow it to spread worldwide to benefit everyone.

Trade... the government of each nation has the obligation to provide the capability within its own country to produce everything possible needed by consumers. Each nation should trade only for what it cannot itself provide or what other nations require that they cannot provide for themselves. The United States has been making trade agreements detrimental to the United States since the Clinton administration and more are proposed. Other nations are doing the same. Each nation is responsible for its own people.

I believe that stability can only be achieved if the world can be divided up into alliances according to common needs, religion, government, economics and trade. These alliances at present would need to be able to defend themselves against predator nations. In my book, titled *Past, Present, and Future of Planet Earth*, I suggest that such alliances are necessary until the day comes when a vast majority of all people on our planet come to agreement on a common culture and way of life. Globalization is not likely any time soon.

Love,
Lawrence A. Stellato

Love Letter #28:
Population Control

September 9, 2022

Dear America,

I remember that, when I was a child, regardless of educational background, we all seemed to come to know that God created planet Earth and later created mankind and instructed us to "increase and multiply and fill the Earth." Well, perhaps He did not mean up to nearly eight billion people. It is very difficult to know how long intelligent life has been in existence on Earth, but I recently read that some scientist estimated it to be about six thousand years. It is difficult to understand how, despite so many wars which killed so many people, despite famines, plagues and so many tragic calamities that have occurred on the planet, that the population could have reached this level. After all, centuries ago, life was not as comfortable as it is in so many countries today. It was more likely a struggle to survive.

Today, we have the New World Order. The New World Order has been in existence since 1947 when, after World War II, rich and powerful people came to believe that, in order to eliminate future wars that would take place when another Hitler or Napoleon came along to take control of other lands by force, we would have a peaceful coexistence of countries under the influence of the United Nations which was formed at that time.

I'm sure that it was their original intention that this would all happen very peacefully and with agreement of all parties. Surely, everyone would agree that this was in the interest of all nations. Unfortunately, it was not so then and it is still not so now. Even now, it does not appear, in my opinion, that the world is anywhere near agreement to globalize. I think that the powers to be have finally come to the conclusion that it is not going to happen unless they force it to occur. There are still too many despots who run their nations like kingdoms and do not want to be part of any world congregation. There are too many disagreements on how government should rule... democracy, communism or a kingdom ruled with absolute power. People in different nations disagree on how they want to be ruled. It would be necessary to equalize the economies of different nations so that people everywhere would live similarly under rules already created by the United Nations. Steps are already being taken to transfer wealth from the middle class of Western nations in Europe and the United States to other countries. It appears that the only thing that the New World Order is right about is that the planet is overpopulated and steps need to be taken to reduce the population to some level in which all of mankind left on Earth would be able to live in relative comfort. Like knowledge about the New World Order, which remains a mystery to most of the Earth's population, most of mankind does not realize that the planet is overcrowded and that the population will continue to grow if the growth is not in some way stunted.

It certainly does appear that God's mandate to "increase and multiply and fill the Earth" has been completed and it is time for some new mandate. Our powerful lords and masters seem to have come to this realization and have begun to take steps to control population. Unfortunately, these powerful

147

people seem to want to see these very dramatic changes take place immediately. They might reduce population through control over worldwide medical care and causing wars to enforce world domination. Most of mankind would agree that killing people to reduce population and provide a better place for the rest of us to live would be wrong. I do not think our lords and masters agree. This is similar to how world leaders want to see fossil fuels eliminated from use on Earth tomorrow, but they have no intention of asking us if we agree or even if we think these changes are necessary. Changes of this magnitude will dramatically affect the lives of everyone on the planet for the worse and cost many trillions of dollars.

Reduction in population of the planet can certainly be achieved. And it certainly can be achieved in a reasonable and legal long-term way. But I do not believe that would satisfy the New World Order. They are taking steps right now, in my opinion, to reduce the number of people on Earth. I believe they are creating a World Health Organization to take control over the health of the entire planet under the auspices of improving the health of everyone. Instead, I have read that the leaders of health organizations are creating hundreds of biology laboratories around the planet that are being used to create viruses that will be spread worldwide. The first was COVID which I believe, as most people do, was created in a laboratory. Then injections are created for the purpose of prevention. These are not technically vaccinations and there appears to be evidence that they are not very effective in preventing the virus. But there is also evidence that people who receive the vaccinations die of other afflictions. None of this is absolutely proven, of course but, if it is true, we are murdering people to reduce the population.

For a long time in most countries, we grew up with the belief that the primary goal in our lives was to get married and have a family. Mankind would continue on our planet in an orderly fashion. It has already been tried in China and other places to control population growth by encouraging people to have only one or maximum two children. That did not work well. Population continued to grow. For a long time, we have encouraged terminations of pregnancy, especially in poorer nations. In these nations especially, populations continue to grow. There are some who believe that we should allow mothers to decide to have their children aborted after birth if they feel they cannot raise them properly. At some point in childbirth and certainly after birth, of course, all of this is murder. It appears that none of this has reduced the population. It is only recently since the introduction of the first virus, that the population has been slightly reduced.

Recently, major changes in education are occurring and are being encouraged. We are beginning to teach our children that gender is not a fact, but a choice. I recently read an article in which the author stated that he believed that there are not two, but seven or eight genders. We are teaching children now as young as three and four years old that they can choose what gender they want to be regardless of whether they were born a boy or a girl. In my opinion, of course, this is totally stupid and I do not believe that practically anyone on Earth wants their children to learn this, but our lords and masters have taken control of our educational system.

The family life that I grew up with in the 1950s is, of course, totally gone. The whole idea of a husband and wife living in the same household with their own children is practically nonexistent today. And the idea that everyone should get married and have children when they grow up is certainly obsolete. But what they want to teach our children in school today to achieve population reduction is total nonsense. I do believe that we are all born with a number of innate different sexual orientations. More men than we think are born with an innate sexual attraction for and a desire for a relationship with another man. It is in their DNA. they should not be chastised for their tendencies and required to marry and have children. The same is true of more women than we think. They should not be required to deny their tendencies. These relationships of men with men and women with women are not marriages. A marriage is a relationship of a man with a woman for the purpose of having and raising children to be responsible adults. Nevertheless, we should recognize relationships of men with men and women with women as being normal. This proper understanding of the way we all are truly created would go a long way toward reducing our overpopulated planet in the long run. It just may not happen as quickly as we would like.

We have long recognized birth control as a method of preventing our children from getting pregnant while they are too young and unable to raise a child. Birth control measures should continue to be encouraged and should be recognized by all religions as a means of maintaining stable worldwide population. Prosperous nations that have adopted and encouraged birth control measures have been experiencing reductions in their native populations. The populations of these countries only keep growing because they are allowing legal and illegal immigration.

Methods of controlling population growth that are reasonable and legal do exist and they will work. We may not see the dramatic and immediate reduction in population that we would like, but it will happen. We should not insist on reducing the number of people on Earth rapidly by control over health and by confusing our children with phony education that is unnecessary. If our world leaders insist on proceeding in their current manner, they may one day be defending themselves against charges of crimes against humanity. It would be totally unnecessary because population reduction can be achieved without harming anyone.

Love,
Lawrence A. Stellato

Love Letter #29:
Goals of the New World Order

September 19, 2022

Dear America,

It is gradually becoming more common knowledge that, beginning in 1947 with the creation of the United Nations, many leaders and wealthy individuals worldwide have been making efforts to unite all of the nations of the world under the direction and control of the United Nations. This effort is often referred to as The New World Order or The Great Reset. In the seventy-five years since this effort began, very many young people from wealthy and powerful families and educated at prestigious universities have been invited to join secret organizations and been indoctrinated in this effort. Very many of them, because of their educational backgrounds and capabilities have been infiltrated into important government and corporate positions worldwide including the media. Although there are likely differences in their opinions on what direction to follow on many issues, they are apparently united in their belief in a world under one universal control created by their design. Though we may have never been invited to their meetings and been made aware of their ideas for our future, it is important for all of us to attempt to understand what they have in store for planet Earth and what their goals might be. The letter that follows contains my own speculations about the history and intent of this effort.

If we are to understand the goals of the New World Order, we should first attempt to understand the history and background that existed at the time which might motivate people to desire to achieve such a lofty goal. It was well known at the time that all previous major civilizations had been formed by conquest and ruled under military control as kingdoms throughout the entire history of the planet. In fact, the world had just defeated an effort by Germany and Japan to gain control of nearly the entire world militarily in World War II. Previous history tells us of the original Egyptians, the Greeks and Spartans, Genghis Khan, the Roman Empire, Napoleon, and Great Britain at one time which had military presence in many nations around the world including the colonies in the new world. There was also World War I. It surely seemed a good idea at the time to create a world organization that might create rules under which all nations on Earth might live in peaceful coexistence. This was the backdrop for the United Nations. Even then, however, problems existed which perhaps escaped their foresight that might prevent the success of this effort.

In my first book, titled *Past, Present, and Future of Planet Earth*, there is a discussion about wars and the reasons that there have been so many wars since intelligent life began here. Perhaps our leaders in 1947, who had such beneficial hopes for the future, did not understand how deep rooted many of the reasons for conflict and war on planet Earth are, and how difficult it might be to encourage or even force people to accept one rule or way of life forced upon them by a United Nations authority. Seventy-five years have passed. Progress has been made, but I fear that these leaders and their apostles have long since come to realize that the entire planet will not voluntarily come under their control and that, therefore, they have begun to attempt to enforce compliance. To understand whether this goal can ever be achieved, we must examine the deep-rooted causes of friction and conflict on our planet. Can mankind be forced to come to agreement on such deep-rooted disagreements?

Racial prejudice is considered by many leaders to be the most outstanding difference. It is my opinion, that there is a great deal of misunderstanding about racial disparity. There appears to have been three basic races of people created in three separate and distinct areas of the planet... black, white and yellow. Whether it happened in a good or bad way, white and black people have become racially mixed for many centuries. There are brown people that resulted from this interracial mix everywhere on Earth, and this happened long before any of us here on Earth today were born. It appears to be historical fact. Forcing integration to happen faster than it chooses to is just cause for further unnecessary friction. Even some Asian people have moved from Asian nations and mixed interracially with white and black people in some locations. I believe the only place on Earth where there has been no integration is in the Asian world. To my knowledge, no white, black or brown person has ever been fully integrated into Asian society, become a citizen there, allowed to own property, marry and have children who would become Asian citizens, run for public office and become part of government in China or Japan. Those privileges are apparently only allowed in white countries. Racial conflict has taken place on our planet in past history. Mainland China is growing economically and militarily very quickly as a result of a transfer of middle-class wealth from the United States and Western Europe resulting from trade agreements made over twenty years ago. China has often stated their goal of gaining control over all Chinese people and will control over a quarter of the world's population soon. Will World War III be fought someday to prevent Oriental control over the entire planet? Many are well aware of China's aspirations to enhance its influence around the world.

World history tells us that we will never run out of people who believe that they have the right to control everything and tell everyone what to do and how to live. The very existence of the New World Order should convince us that this is true. Planet Earth still contains many nations that are run like kingdoms. Many Middle Eastern nations, African nations and Latin American countries are essentially ruled by dictators who will be extremely reluctant to turn over control of their people and wealth to the United Nations. Many nations will join if it seems to be for their benefit but, when asked to turn over their wealth for the benefit of others as is being done in the United States and Western Europe today, they will balk. It is my opinion that it would take a great many wars to force all nations on the planet to submit control to the United Nations. Even greater nations may not submit. We must ask if Vladimir Putin is right now trying to rebuild the Soviet empire that once existed so that he would be able economically and militarily to resist control by the United Nations? Will China, which is growing more powerful militarily and economically, submit to U.N. demands to relinquish their newfound wealth to poorer nations when ordered to do so by the United Nations?

A couple of centuries ago, revolutions overturned the rule of some kingdoms in Europe. Democracy and communism were born out of the desire of the people to have the right to vote for the leaders who will rule them. Communism took hold primarily in Russia and China where leaders in this movement are very devout and appear extremely dedicated to spreading communism and their own influence around the world. Democratic governments took hold in many European countries and especially in the United States. Conflict and war to prevent the spread of communism worldwide has erupted in several areas of the world. The United Nations appears to be siding with the spread of communism which will provide more complete control of government over the people. All ten leaders of the UN to date have been radical socialists or communists. Eradication of democracy and capitalism in the United States will likely guarantee eventual communist control worldwide. Communism is nothing more than total socialism which does not allow ownership of property, wealth or capital by the people except as allowed and controlled by the government. Communism is the easiest way for government to have total control over the lives of the people, and eradication of democratic freedoms and capitalism is the easiest way to achieve it. In reality, capitalism is probably responsible for practically all of the gains achieved for a better life by all of mankind. It is also likely, therefore, that eliminating capitalism will lead to the downfall of Western civilization and herald the coming of a thousand years of dark ages such as was experienced after the downfall of the Roman Empire.

Trade agreements have proven to have enormous power to transfer wealth from prosperous nations to poorer nations. Such trade agreements, which have become and are becoming more popular, are being used as a tool by the leaders of the New World Order and the U.N. to transfer wealth and military power among nations at will, and we will see more of them. Such disproportionate treatment of nations by those who see themselves as our overlords can result in major additional conflict and war worldwide because it affects the lives of so many who have achieved success so dramatically and distributes wealth to those who fail to achieve it.

The leaders of the New World Order, I believe, also see the population of the planet as having grown too large and too rapidly. About this, they are correct. It is easy to see that it is very likely impossible to provide a decent life for nearly eight billion people on the planet with the resources that exist here. They appear to be attempting to reduce the population by taking control of health resources worldwide and education of children worldwide. Population does have to be reduced, but it is my understanding that possibly dangerous and illegal methods will be used to accomplish this goal. It is, in my opinion, totally unnecessary. I believe population control is achievable and it can be reduced long term in a very reasonable way.

The problems described in this essay describe major impediments to achieving the long-term goals of the New World Order at any time in the near-term future. People are very passionate about religion. Attempting to eliminate religion from their lives or throwing people of all religions together in the same place is likely to increase friction and possibly war. Asking despots to relinquish their power is futile. It will take many wars to force them into submission and great military strength to continue to enforce control over the many nations which are likely to resist. In many nations, it is not only the leaders who will resist. The people will also not want to give over control to a U.N. that has the interest of other nations at heart. Democracy and communism are diametrically opposed government systems. Trying to force people to completely change their way of life in such dramatic fashion would seem likely to cause revolution in many places. You will be putting people in the military in the position of having to kill their own neighbors to maintain order. Trade agreements becoming more common that redistribute wealth from some nations to others are about the most unfair thing that a leader can do to his own people. Redistributing wealth through socialist policies within nations is just as unfair. Such redistribution can cause great unrest within and between nations. Transferring economic power to aggressive nations can cause additional friction and war. Even the fact of the existence of a world body attempting to control the planet can cause world leaders to take aggressive action to put their nations in a position to resist control by the United Nations. The additional effort to install a central bank digital currency, which has already been done in China and is being attempted in the United States, establishes an even more cruel control over the lives of the people by government. I cannot imagine total acceptance by people worldwide of such a measure is achievable. No one will want to live that way.

It is my opinion that the world is nowhere near ready to accept total U.N. control or any such globalization effort. Continuation of such efforts, in my opinion, will only lead to increased conflict and war. To achieve worldwide peaceful coexistence, I think the best current possible solution was suggested by George Orwell in his book, "1984." The world needs to be divided up into nations which have common interests... similar religion, similar government, similar social structure and economics, perhaps a similar racial structure as appears to be necessary in the Oriental countries. These nations can form alliances with other nations of similar interest and should be left alone by other nations to live life in their own way without interference. What we really need to eliminate is the desire of the wealthy and powerful to feel that they have the right to rule over everyone and tell everybody how to live. They do not have that right and they are the ultimate cause of all friction and war.

Love,
Lawrence A. Stellato

Love Letter #30:
Open Borders

October 7, 2022

Dear America,

I guess people have been coming to America since 1492, when it was first discovered by Christopher Columbus. After achieving independence from Great Britain and writing the Constitution in 1776, the United States of America became an independent nation, presumably with closed borders except for legal immigration. Surely, it was determined that only legal immigration would be sanctioned in order that immigrants could be screened to prevent disease and enemy antagonists from freely entering the country. As the American economy grew because it became the home of freedom, democracy and capitalism, many more people have desired to come to America. Freedom, democracy and capitalism originally only existed and grew in Western Europe and the United States in the last two centuries or so. It was the first time in all of planet Earth that any such thing had ever been seen because all previous societies were ruled as kingdoms on this planet since the dawn of mankind. Even Communist countries, which do allow citizens to vote for their leaders do not allow ownership of wealth, property or capital to citizens except as permitted by government. Word spread worldwide that America was the land

160

of opportunity. Eventually, as democracy and capitalism grew in Western Europe, European immigration to the United States slowed.

For a long time, illegal immigration was substantially contained. But we have always allowed legal immigration. The goal, of course, was to not only prevent disease but also to insure that people coming here would be able to support themselves or be taken care of by family, and would not become a substantial burden on the American people. This system worked well for a very long time. But since 1947, we now have the New World Order. Although the leaders of this movement to change the world may have all accumulated their own wealth because of capitalism, they condemn American democracy and capitalism as being a very unfair system, and apparently their goal is to eradicate our American way of life. They feel that Americans and Europeans should not have a better life than people in Asia, Africa or Latin America or other places, and that it is their obligation to take wealth from these nations and distribute it more equally to all. Just as exists in Communist countries, however, these wealthy leaders do not intend to redistribute their own wealth and agree to live in poverty with the rest of us. But they feel that the great middle class achieved by the developed nations as they are called should be redistributed to poorer nations.

These wealthy and powerful elites who are planning our future are not without plans for achieving their goals. They have long-established worldwide trade organizations which have been changing trade practices worldwide. During the Clinton administration, free trade was opened between the United States and Europe with China and India. In the last twenty years, these new agreements have transferred many millions of jobs from the more prosperous developed nations to China and India which has the ability to transfer huge amounts of middle-class wealth to the developing nations. The United States has had trade deficits with other nations averaging probably about a trillion dollars a year for likely about the last thirty or forty years. This transfer of wealth is a direct result of changes in trade practices. Americans were not properly advised of what the result of these changes would be and no one asked them if they agreed. Even today, it is unlikely that most Americans understand the impact these changes in trade agreements have had on our nation. We make nothing in the United States anymore and our young people are asked to make a career at McDonalds for lack, in many cases, of a better place to work.

Another method of equalizing wealthy status of nations is through immigration. In the last decade or two, many millions of Middle Easterners have been allowed to emigrate illegally into European nations. From all appearances, the population of these European nations were generally not in favor of these changes, but their leaders are all members, for the most part, of this elitist group, and they do not ask the people they rule to participate in these decisions. Elitists know we will not agree to changes they are making which are obviously not in the best interest of our own nations. They are worldwide equalization goals. They have also simply opened up the borders here in the United States to anyone worldwide. The current administration is presently allowing the equivalent of about two million illegals a year into this country. There has never been any discussion about the incredible cost to Europeans or Americans to support and integrate these illegals.

The cost is not just monetary. Europe has always been a Christian country, at least for about two thousand years.

Muslims coming into Europe do not leave their Muslim religion behind. As they also do in the Middle East, Muslims take over towns and villages often militarily. When they do this, they always gain control over the local government and it is their intention to change the local way of life as far as possible to Sharia law. You may not read about it in the newspapers, but unrest has spread substantially throughout Europe because Muslims do not integrate easily into society. Towns and villages in the United States have also been substantially changed to an extent because many Muslims have settled here. Changes have taken place here more in Michigan and Minnesota likely than anywhere else. In the United States, more than anywhere else, immigrants are from Latin America. They are poor, have to be housed and integrated, and the cost will be in the many billions. The overall average middle class will surely be substantially reduced. Is it not likely that, in the long run, people here will not become much more distressed over the poverty which will become much more widespread because of the changes being made? Will class struggle result? Is more racial division being encouraged by the government?

As stated earlier, the overall goal of the New World Order is merely to equalize worldwide status under their control. They do not seem to understand much about or care much about the reasons for conflict and war which have plagued planet Earth since the dawn of mankind. Religion, taking control over other people's land and changing society in which people live without their consent are the major reasons for conflict and war throughout the history of the world. Trade policy is becoming the next major change which will cause conflict and war. The elites are throwing us together as a melting pot perhaps expecting that they are going to be in full control over our lives anyway, and they are not going to allow us to fight over or have any choice in how we choose to live or what religion we follow.

It is my opinion that the New World Order will not succeed. It is not just the huge redistribution of wealth that they are causing. It is not just the internal distress within nations that they are encouraging. It is not just that they do not seem to understand how deep the religious differences are and that people cannot accept the changes. They also seem to fail to understand that people care deeply about the type of government they want to live under and the type of society in which they choose to live. There are still many nations on planet Earth that are ruled as kingdoms. How can we get a king to give over his nation to be ruled by the United Nations? I assume they expect to do it by force. It will mean many wars. Is Vladimir Putin right now trying to rebuild his empire to include everything he needs to keep his people free from control by the United Nations? China, for the time being, seems to have accepted capitalism into its society because it is in its best interest to do so. But no Communist country in the history of planet Earth has accepted a democratic and capitalist way of life. Communists do not give up their total control of the population. Will China, as it becomes wealthier, give up control to the United Nations, which will demand that it agree to share its newfound wealth with the rest of the world? China will balk and resist control by the United Nations. China right now is the most aggressive nation on planet Earth and seeks ever more power on its own. Like all other Communist nations have in the past, China could take control and ownership of all capital provided to it by other nations. Control over the population is paramount in Communist nations.

I believe that people still want to come to the United States because they believe it is still the land of opportunity, freedom and democracy and the American dream. Nothing could be further from the truth. The United States today is ruled by the New World Order and has been for many years. With the exception of Ronald Reagan and Donald Trump, all of the presidents of the United States have been in favor of a united planet since John F. Kennedy. All departments of our government have been infiltrated with people trying to change our way of life without our knowledge. We still have the Constitution, but our government is disregarding it constantly and the Judicial Department will not uphold it any longer. Joe Biden has recently introduced an executive order to change the U.S. dollar to a central bank digital currency. When that takes place, freedom and democracy disappear from the United States forever. And when they have full control over all Americans, capitalism will likely disappear.

It is a great gift that we still have some leaders here in America which believe in our great American way of life and would work diligently to preserve it for the American people. We must return control over our government to these conservatives who are primarily Republican. Voting is difficult. Lying has become so commonplace. Certainly, anyone who wants to open the borders of the United States to allow anyone worldwide to come here illegally does not have the best interest of the people of this country at heart and should not be president of the United States. One of the most important goals we must demand of our leaders is that they want to close American borders to illegal immigration and allow only legal immigrants into our country. We can no longer vote by party affiliation. We must now learn to understand which candidates still believe in the American dream and will help the United States resist control by those who would enslave us and return the country to the nation it was intended to be by our forefathers, who wrote the original Constitution.

Love,
Lawrence A. Stellato

Love Letter #31:
The Proper Use of Capital

November 15, 2022

Dear America,

Only in a democratic country are ordinary citizens allowed to own property, accumulate wealth, and accumulate and use capital. That is why capitalism was born in democratic nations. We all know that citizens of Communist countries are not allowed to accumulate wealth or employ capital to produce products. If you invent a product that can be useful to many people and use your own money or funds from others to produce that product and sell it to others, you are employing capital as intended and our system of capitalism is designed to reward you for your efforts to help make life better for others. This is proper use of capital in a capitalist system. But it is unfortunately not what we do in the United States any more. To begin with, practically nothing we use, drive or even most of what we eat is not produced in this country any more. Although products may be being produced using American capital, almost everything is produced overseas and shipped back to us.

American capital used to produce products should be employed right here in the U.S., creating career jobs for Americans, especially as it pertains to energy, food, and military supplies. What do we use capital in the United States for? A great deal of American capital has been employed to create Facebook, Google, and the internet. While these are useful for entertainment purposes, they produce no tomatoes, potatoes or washing machines. Movies and other entertainment venues are necessary, but it seems that is all we employ capital for these days in America. Hundreds of billions, if not trillions, of dollars today are employed to purchase cryptocurrencies. Many billions more are planned for creation of a metaverse. These are nothing more than entries on someone's computer. Often, we do not even know whose computer it is. How inflationary is it that capital we need to produce the products we need and use every day is not available for that purpose and is being utilized elsewhere. How much of the capital invested in the stock market today is used for the creation of entertainment venues instead of products and services for consumers? Investment managers, fearful of recession, are diverting capital away from needy young companies which will be improving the lives of Americans in the future.

I fear that we are drifting further and further away from the intended use of capital, which has been responsible for the creation of almost everything that has been invented to improve the lives of citizens worldwide over the last two hundred years. It does not bode well for the future of mankind.

Love,
Lawrence A. Stellato

Love Letter #32:
Is Global Warming a Hoax?

November 29, 2022

Dear America,

When I was young in the 1950s and 1960s, I do remember a lot of discussion about dirty air and water that was a side effect of the industrial revolution and manufacturing that was taking place primarily in the United States and Western Europe at the time. There was also a lot of discussion about the icebergs melting in the Artic and the anticipated effect this global warming would have in the future. Predictions were made that Florida and the West Coast of California would be underwater by the year 2000. The scientists were good at science. Their prediction came true. But they were not good at math, and it did not cause the flooding that was predicted. Air did become dirty, and water did become polluted. A great deal has changed in the U.S. and Europe in my lifetime. Manufacturing all went overseas to other countries. Governments, especially in the United States, made major efforts to clean up the air and water with great success. There was also great success in learning how to manufacture and build and provide energy in a cleaner way with respect for the environment. Most of today's pollution is in other countries. No one would argue that we must continuously strive for cleaner air and water on the planet. It is also true that the planet is one to two degrees warmer today than it was years ago. All scientists do know, however, that this is not a major climate event on planet Earth compared to so many dramatic changes that have taken place here over many centuries. They are just not talking about it.

Not all scientists agree that the planet is dying because of global warming. Some do not even agree that it is warming. Not long ago, I read a report published by a group of scientists who stated that, over the last few hundred years, there is evidence that the Earth has gone through a number of warming and cooling cycles. Each warming or cooling cycle lasts about seventy or eighty years. They claim that we are just ending a warming cycle and entering a cooling cycle. These scientists have seen evidence that ice is accumulating again in Antarctica and that certain places on Earth are beginning to get cooler again. This evidence appears to be confirmed by my own life experience. I do remember that places in the northern United States in which I lived over sixty years ago were very cold and have gotten warmer since. But in the last five years, it has occurred to me that winters have started to get colder again. In my opinion, there is no reason that the planet, in its orbit around the sun, cannot get a bit closer or further away every seventy or eighty years, resulting in a slight temperature change. This suggests that it may not be mankind's use of fossil fuels that is causing the temperature change. I do believe that the use of fossil fuels does make our air and water dirtier and that we should be cleaning up after ourselves. But I do not believe that our use of fossil fuels is warming the climate and I also do not believe that the planet is going to become uninhabitable because of planet warming. I do believe that planet warming and cooling as well as many other much more dramatic changes have been happening on our planet since the dawn of time and that we will still be here for many centuries to come regardless.

We do not have to make major changes to our lifestyle as is being planned for us. The next five to ten years will show how unnecessary the many trillions of dollars we are spending and the vast reductions in lifestyle we are imposing on the population will prove to be. I do believe that some of our world leaders do believe the climate change hoax and are acting in good faith when they change our lives to compensate. But I also believe that there are many others who know climate change is not a danger to mankind and are simply using it to change our way of life, redistribute wealth and gain greater control over mankind.

Love,
Lawrence A. Stellato

Love Letter #33:
The Future of Planet Earth

December 4, 2022

Dear America,

Our world has undergone so many changes since the end of World War II. It became divided up between the East and the West... communism and democracy. There was a Cold War during which wars were fought to contain the spread of communism from China into Korea and Vietnam. The Russian Communist Empire contained half of Germany and all the eastern nations of Europe. The Russian Empire collapsed during the Reagan Administration as Eastern European nations chose democracy. Socialism has grown dramatically throughout Europe and Latin America. Trade agreements made in Western Europe and the United States have transferred very substantial wealth from the middle classes of those countries to China, India and other nations, increasing the economic and military power of Communist and Islamic nations, especially China and Iran. Most importantly of all, the United Nations, which was created in 1947 after World War II, began an effort over many years to bring the world together under control of the United Nations. Originally, world leaders likely expected that all nations would agree to become members voluntarily and see the benefits of world peace and unity that could result.

Perhaps it escaped their notice that there are too many differences in religion and type of government and society in which people choose to live to get them all living in harmony. After many centuries, people are still killing each other over these ideologies. The history of our planet is not a history of mankind, it is a history of conflict and war. Nevertheless, the United Nations and the New World Order or the New Reset as it is called, has grown substantially in power and control unnoticed. It appears to have decided that all nations must be brought under the control of the U.N. by force if necessary, since many nations will not choose to comply. Up until the present, the United States has been the center of democracy and capitalism. But in the last fifty years or so, all elected presidents of the United States with the exception of Ronald Reagan and Donald Trump have been supporters of the U.N. and the New World Order. Under the circumstances, the United States has become sort of the military arm of the United Nations to try to enforce world compliance for unity under U.N. control. It is noteworthy that all U.N. leaders to date have been radical Socialists or Communists. We must conclude, therefore, that the United Nations' control over planet Earth will result in a Totalitarian State. So many changes have taken place that, with the exception of the elitists and government officials who have engineered these changes, few people on our planet truly understand what is taking place. Where will all of this take us? What is the future of planet Earth?

If we are to attempt to predict the future, we must first understand the ideologies that divide us. Wars fought to contain dictators who attempt to take control of other lands and people are likely the primary reason that the history of mankind is a history of conflict and war. It is not likely that we will ever run out of people with huge egos that feel they have the right to tell everybody where and how to live. The entire New World Order movement today is entirely made up of such people. Wars over religion are legendary. Movies have been made about them. The spread of Islam worldwide has only begun. Muslims take their religion wherever they go, take control of local governments, and change society to suit them. Jews have relocated to many Christian areas of the world and take Judaism wherever they go. Although Christianity did not originally spread militarily, Christianity has allied with governments since the Holy Roman Empire to influence rules of society. Religion is the source of all ethics and morality and therefore has substantial influence on the rules of our society. What is legal and what is moral or ethical is decided by religious beliefs. Communism and democracy are diametrically opposed types of government. Socialism and capitalism are very different types of society. How likely is it that we will no longer fight wars over how our government and society operate? Elites and government officials have used new types of trade agreements to transfer vast amounts of wealth from richer to poorer nations. Expansion of such rules will increase the prospect of conflict and war in our future. How likely is it that aristocrats will throw all these people with all these different ideas that we kill each other over every day into the same pot and expect peace and harmony? Some are already predicting that World War III will be the result of this effort by the New World Order to enforce universal compliance under United Nations control.

If we are to attempt to predict what will happen in the future of our planet, we will need to look at the various sections of Earth and understand what the future of each section might be. We start at home. Major efforts are being made worldwide to destroy democracy and capitalism in the United States as well as everywhere else in the world. The right to own property, the means of production and accumulate wealth only exists in a democratic capitalist society. Such rights have to be eliminated for a totalitarian communist type of society that will rule the world to be created. If these rights are lost in the United States, America and Europe become the center for the promotion of worldwide totalitarian control. The United States must become once again the center for the preservation of democracy and capitalism on planet Earth. This nation could ensure its capability to remain independent of world control by taking certain steps to preserve its future. The United States could leave the United Nations and absorb or form alliances with all nations in the western hemisphere and thereby preserve the existence of democracy and capitalism throughout the hemisphere. Within this area, there exists adequate supplies of food, energy, manufacturing capability and military capability to insure independence for the entire area.

Communist China has grown substantially in economic and military power as a result of trade agreements made with the United States and Europe which have transferred vast amounts of middle-class wealth from those countries to China. Communist China apparently fully intends to gain absolute control over the entire oriental world. China has accepted, for the time being, partial capitalism. It is noteworthy, however, that no Communist country on planet Earth has tolerated capitalism indefinitely. I believe that, when capitalism has served its purpose there, China will nationalize all foreign assets as all other Communist countries have in the past. I do not see how Communists can tolerate ownership of capital and means of production by the people. The people cannot be allowed to have that kind of power in a Communist society. China's middle class is becoming quite wealthy. When the leaders of the New World Order order China to redistribute this newfound wealth to other poorer nations as the United States and Europe have done, China will balk. China will no longer need the United Nations and is not likely to submit formally to U.N. rule. China intends to gain absolute control over all oriental lands and will even eventually move against Japan. This oriental conglomerate will have total capability to provide its own food, manufacturing capability and military strength, but needs to also supply its energy needs and will likely therefore ally with middle eastern nations.

Russian communism is not the same as China's. Russia has not installed a central bank digital currency and may not intend to exercise as much control over its people as exists in China where there is a central bank digital currency or where it is intended in the United States and Europe. I believe that Russia is right now trying to extend its influence into Ukraine which can insure food supply. Russia will then ensure its own food, energy, manufacturing and military strength and be able also to resist United Nations control. The United States appears to have become the military arm of the United Nations at present and is trying to prevent Russian control of Ukraine. The United States and the U.N. want Ukraine to join the United Nations. Eastern European nations will have to choose between Russia and the U.N. Either way, they will live in a Communist or Totalitarian state.

Other sections of the world will also have to choose. I do not believe that either India or the Middle Eastern nations would accept total control by the United Nations as intended in a Totalitarian state. It remains to be seen how some sections of the world might be able to accumulate the capability to become totally independent and provide for their own needs or they might have to comply with U.N. control. If an honest poll was taken today to determine whether the eight billion people on Earth would choose government control and equality or freedom and independence and equality of opportunity, I believe not many would opt for total government control. That is why freedom of speech must be controlled and the press worldwide must be complicit in this effort. The world is not going to be given the option of how they choose to live.

The question now remains: will the United States and the United Nations continue to pursue its objective to control the planet despite opposition? If it does, there will be World War III. Too many nations which have the capability to remain independent will not comply. The world is not ready for globalization or for voluntary unification. There remain too many differences in the way people choose to live, and they should be allowed to live as they choose. So, the answer to a peaceful planet at present is division into sections of nations with common interests. The elites on Earth have the capability to help the world sectionalize in a way that it makes sense and there could be peace and prosperity, and they must start to think in that direction. Someday, the population of planet Earth may come to an agreement on the best way for all of us to live. We won't be here to see it, but we can plant the seeds and ideas for the future. In the meantime, we must create a world in which people can all live in an area that enables them to be with others that have common interests and beliefs.

Love,
Lawrence A. Stellato

Epilogue

It is true that, because they created democracy and capitalism, citizens of the United States of America and Western Europe have enjoyed economic progress and prosperity substantially in excess of many other areas of the planet. It is not true that the prosperous nations developed by stealing resources from other countries. It is not true that the prosperous nations developed by taking advantage of poorer countries or enslaving them. It is not true that the developed nations have any particular prejudice against any race or religion or would in any way prevent any other nation from developing itself because of prejudice. It is, in fact, more likely true that the United States and Western Europe have, for a couple of centuries, attempted to spread democracy and capitalism to many other nations with the intention of improving the lives of the people in poorer nations. Practically all of the wealth in the Middle East, which is unfortunately mostly hoarded by the wealthy, was made by selling petroleum products to the West, sometimes at truly exorbitant prices. Japan and South Korea certainly improved the lives of their citizens by doing business with the West. China, India, Canada, and Mexico are all presently enjoying very favorable trade arrangements with the United States, which are vastly improving the middle classes of those countries. How unfair is it to continue to condemn the United States for being unfair to the world after practically every area of planet Earth has achieved some level of improvement in society because of the spread of democracy and capitalism around the globe?

The United States is under attack verbally and economically by global elites because it is necessary for them to destroy the Constitution of our country for them to gain control over and enslave the entire population of the world. Our Constitution gives people rights that the global elites do not want us to have. We have the right to own property and accumulate wealth. We were given the right to free speech which has already been taken away from us. Our own government is trying to install laws to make it possible to cheat in elections and take away our right to vote so that they can control who will be in office. It is my belief that the forefathers of this great nation gave us two primary gifts that were intended to protect us forever from the government control enjoyed by kingdoms since the dawn of time. They gave citizens the right to vote in lawful elections to decide who should rule them. Many efforts are taking place today in this country to take away this great gift which is so necessary to prevent Totalitarian government control over our lives. Our great forefathers in America gave us the greatest gift of all... equal opportunity. Equal opportunity has never existed on planet Earth before. It means that we have the right to own property and the means of production and accumulate wealth. Equality is stressed as the goal of a fair society. Equality for everybody is communism. And it is certainly not what our founders of this great country intended for us. Even Communist countries today do not have the equality that was intended by the original Communist leaders. Government officials and elites authorized by government to manage production and distribution for the government do not live according to the same standards afforded to workers in Communist countries. Equality of opportunity is what was intended for us. The United States gave up equality of opportunity when it created the prejudice laws of the 1960s. Rules were created at that time to grant favoritism in education at all levels, in all government programs and in private industry jobs to certain groups of people. Favoritism is mandated to all non-white people. Favoritism is granted to all non-Christians. Favoritism is granted to all women over men. More recently, favoritism is now granted to all people who have special sexual preferences. Special considerations have long been given to illegal immigrants who get free medical attention and other benefits not granted to citizens. Who can deny that the group most prejudiced against on all of planet Earth is white, European, Christian, non-homophobic, male citizens of this country. Favoritism to certain groups has been going on and expanding in America for about seventy years.

The changes that are occurring in the United States which are destroying our intended American way of life are encouraged, but not caused by, very powerful foreign elites and politicians. But they are being made by our own leaders. In my *Love Letters to America*, I stress in several places that many of America's leaders in our lifetimes are very much in favor of a unified world under the direction of the United Nations. This does include Presidents Jimmy Carter, George H. W. Bush, George W. Bush, Bill Clinton, Barack Obama and certainly Joe Biden. Only Ronald Reagan and Donald Trump violently opposed the subjugation of the United States to the United Nations and the New World Order. I suspect that Richard Nixon also opposed globalization and that is why he was so persecuted for so minimal a crime in which he had no part and likely did not even sanction. By and large, the media is complicit in this effort, but you can go into any Barnes and Noble or other bookstore and find books that will identify world elites and their intention for the New World Order, or Great Reset, as it is often called.

A unified world would not be a bad idea if it intended to grant a better way of life to the population of Earth. Unfortunately, that is not what is intended. What is planned for us is a totalitarian form of government far worse than exists today in communism. Such a world cannot include free elections, free speech, individual ownership of wealth, property or means of production. In the entire history of planet Earth, we only have these rights for the last couple of centuries. We will not only lose these rights, but technology has now been developed which will also give the government the capability to create a central bank digital currency which will give government absolute control over every aspect of our lives by control over our money and how much we have and how we spend it. We are headed to a world that is as bad as the original control under kingdoms.

We are drifting rapidly further and further away from the America that was created by our great forefathers who wrote the Constitution and created the greatest society that ever existed for mankind on planet Earth. I am saddened that so many leaders, elites and politicians would favor the creation of the world that they have planned for us. I am devastated that Americans could be so complacent and unknowing as to allow and actually vote for the changes occurring in America that could eventually result in their enslavement by their own government. My heart is broken over the loss of what our forefathers fought so hard to gain for us when they created our great society.

I make my *Love Letters to America* available today in the hope that they will someday be widely read and help Americans and perhaps many others in the world aware of the greatness that America was intended to be. I hope it will help people understand the gift it presented not only to America, but potentially the world. Only through democracy and capitalism can the world become a better place to live for all humanity. There are problems, but they can be solved. The very elites who would enslave humanity have the power to make the world a better place by adopting the more humanitarian and conservative economic principles the world needs to become a better place. It is my sincere hope that I am contributing in some small way to this effort.